"Do you know wh☑ **W9-APL-894** **night in Vegas?" he asked in a rough voice.**

"More than waking up married to the woman who got your car towed?"

He chuckled, a deep and throaty sound that made her want to arch her body against his. His hands on her arms weren't enough anymore. She wanted to feel them *everywhere*.

"Maybe even more than that," he confirmed. "I hate that I had you in my bed and don't remember every single second of it."

The constant ache for his touch flared into a hunger she couldn't resist anymore, and she stepped closer. His hands slid up her arms to her shoulders as she moved, one continuing up to cup the back of her neck.

"Just to be clear," she said. "I had *you* in *my* bed."

"Your room was closer to the elevator. I probably couldn't wait until the end of the hall."

Chelsea ran her fingertip down his throat to the dip below his Adam's apple. "Sounds like you were pretty hot for a woman you didn't like very much."

"As I recall, that feeling was mutual. You told Laura Thompson you would duct-tape your knees together before you let me in there."

"One, you weren't supposed to hear that, obviously. And, two, I was drinking coffee when I said that. I was drinking tequila when I forgot it."

"You're sober now."

"Yes, I am. And so are you."

Dear Reader,

Most of the people in my books will get some small piece of their character from somebody I know and love. A dislike of broccoli. A man who loathes being a passenger in any vehicle and gets cranky if he can't drive. (Both of those are from my husband, actually.) Chelsea Grey has been a part of the Sutton's Place world since *Her Hometown Man*, and in *Married by Mistake*, we really get to know her and her craving for a sense of community.

I was raised in the air force, and even when we were stationed in one place for several years, we moved around within the area. Multiple new schools almost every year. Always the new kid. When I moved to this town at eighteen, nobody knew me. I had no childhood friends, just like Chelsea. *Unlike* Chelsea, I did not have a business neighbor I couldn't stand but accidentally woke up married to in Las Vegas! I hope you enjoy reading the story of how Chelsea Grey and John Fletcher, who want very different things in life (and don't like each other at all), find their way to a happily-ever-after.

You can find out what I'm up to and keep up with book news on my website, www.shannonstacey.com, where you'll find the latest information, as well as a link to sign up for my newsletter. I love connecting with readers, so you'll also find links to where I can be found on social media.

Welcome back to Sutton's Place, and happy reading!

Shannon

Married by Mistake

SHANNON STACEY

HARLEQUIN
SPECIAL
EDITION

HARLEQUIN®
SPECIAL
EDITION™

Recycling programs
for this product may
not exist in your area.

ISBN-13: 978-1-335-59443-3

Married by Mistake

Copyright © 2023 by Shannon Stacey

For questions and comments about the quality of this book, please contact us at CustomerService@Harlequin.com.

Harlequin Enterprises ULC
22 Adelaide St. West, 41st Floor
Toronto, Ontario M5H 4E3, Canada
www.Harlequin.com

Printed in U.S.A.

A *New York Times* and *USA TODAY* bestselling author of over forty romances, **Shannon Stacey** grew up in a military family and lived in many places before landing in a small New Hampshire town where she has resided with her husband and two sons for over twenty years. Her favorite activities are reading and writing with her dogs at her side. She also loves coffee, Boston sports and watching too much TV. You can learn more about her books at www.shannonstacey.com.

Visit the Author Profile page
at Harlequin.com for more titles.

For Lee. Thank you for your friendship, and I hope we're still eating dessert together when we're eighty.

Chapter One

Good morning, Stonefield! Just a reminder the Stonefield Public Library will be closed this weekend because the librarian has run off to Las Vegas to get married! Best wishes to Callan Avery and Molly Cyrs! And a little birdie told us the Perkin' Up Café and Fletcher Digital Restoration and Design are also closed because Chelsea Grey and John Fletcher were invited to witness the happy event. We're hoping what happens in Vegas doesn't stay in Vegas and there will be lots of photos!
      —Stonefield Gazette *Facebook Page*

Before she even opened her eyes, Chelsea Grey knew she wasn't in her own bed. It was the sheets that gave it away. Never in her life had she been able to afford sheets this luxuriously soft.

Las Vegas, she thought. That explained not only the hotel sheets, but also the headache. After flying in from New Hampshire yesterday, she'd gone straight to a prewedding celebration for her friend Molly and her sexy librarian fiancé, Callan.

Chelsea groaned and forced her eyes open. Obviously, she'd celebrated a little too much.

Stretching, she reached for the bottle of water on the nightstand, not caring if it was warm, but a glint of gold stopped her. There was a ring on her left hand—on *that* finger.

Molly's ring.

Yes, Molly had given her the rings before they boarded their flight in Boston and asked her to keep them safe. Chelsea took that responsibility very seriously, but putting Molly's band on her finger seemed like an extreme way to keep from losing it.

Just as she lifted herself onto her right elbow so she could reach the water bottle, the mattress dipped and the soft, expensive sheet slid over her toward the other side of the bed. Dry mouth instantly forgotten, she gasped and sat up, yanking the sheet back and clutching it to her neck.

An extremely handsome man was blinking up at her. His dark hair was tousled—and, *oh no*, she could remember those thick strands sliding through her fingers—and his strong jaw was shadowed by dark stubble. Confusion clouded his bright blue eyes, and the way he winced told her his head wasn't in any better shape than hers.

She was in bed with John Fletcher. Her *nemesis*, if she was feeling dramatic. And right now felt pretty dramatic.

They were naked.

And he was wearing Callan's wedding band.

"Chelsea?" He scrubbed his hand over his face, and that was when he noticed the ring on his finger. "What the hell?"

"Did we get married last night?" How were those words even coming out of her mouth?

"You're naked." He frowned. "*I'm* naked. We're both naked."

She could see that he was naked from the waist up, but she'd really been hoping against hope he had pants on under that sheet.

At least they were in *her* room, she thought, so she was saved a walk of shame through the hotel. John would have that pleasure this morning. But a small, wilted bouquet on the desk caught her eye, and the desire to throw this man out of her room took a backseat to her growing horror. Even from the bed, she could see there were papers next to it that hadn't been on the desk when she left the room to go down for dinner yesterday.

Please don't let that be a marriage certificate.

"I don't understand how I got here," John said, and she told herself she was imagining the hint of accusation in his voice.

Even hungover and confused, he had to know that no matter how desperate Chelsea was to get a man so drunk he'd fall naked into her bed, he would be the very last person she would choose. She didn't even like living in the same town as John Fletcher.

"Okay, let's talk this out," she said, trying to sound calm even though she was one hundred percent freaking out on the inside. "We had dinner and drinks with Molly and Callan."

"Too many drinks on not enough food after too long a flight."

"Then they went up to their room and we sat in awkward silence for a while because they were fixing an error on my bill and you wouldn't leave me by myself. And we drank more because what else is there to do when you're stuck with somebody you don't want to talk to?"

He rolled his eyes at her tone, but nodded. "And then we decided to call a truce for the sake of their wedding."

"I remember that. And the shot to seal the deal." She wasn't much of a drinker, and it was the first time she'd ever done a tequila shot. And that one hadn't been the last. "And then I think we did more shots."

"Neither of us knew how Las Vegas wedding chapels work, so we decided to go check it out. I think. It's pretty fuzzy."

"Very fuzzy. But maybe we did…like a rehearsal. A dress rehearsal, complete with wedding bands."

"With flowers?" he asked, nodding his head toward the desk.

"I don't know what those papers are next to the flowers," she admitted.

"You should go look."

She shook her head, clutching the sheet tighter. "I'm naked. You go."

"I'm naked, too." He flopped back onto the pillow. "I don't think it was a dress rehearsal. It's a blur, but I'm pretty sure we got married last night and then came back here and, uh…consummated the marriage."

Well, they were both naked. And as he spoke, memories flashed through her mind—her hands on his back, his mouth on her breast, her back arching as she gasped his name—leaving little doubt they'd definitely consummated the marriage.

It wouldn't be easy, but she could probably reconcile her dislike of John Fletcher with an alcohol-fueled one-night stand. A woman had needs, after all, and hers had been ignored for a long time. But *marrying* him? Yesterday she would have bet everything she owned there wasn't enough booze in the city.

Then the clock caught her eye and she almost leaped out of the bed before remembering she wasn't wearing pajamas. "We're going to be late to breakfast."

Molly had a full day planned leading up to their ceremony, and the last thing she'd told them before

Callan pulled her away from the table was to *not* be late meeting them at the breakfast buffet.

"I think they'll understand," he said in a droll way that made her want to kick him.

"We're not raining on her wedding-day parade, so we're not going to be late to breakfast and we're definitely not going to tell them what happened the first time we were left alone without supervision. I'm closing my eyes, so get dressed. Quickly."

The mattress dipped as John slid out of her bed, and she listened to him hunting for and putting on yesterday's clothes. She was tempted to peek, but she resisted and kept her eyes closed until she heard the rustle of papers. John was reading the documents from the table.

"It's official. We got married last night." He tossed the papers next to the dying flowers and looked at her, his brow creased with confusion. "But I don't even *like* you."

"I don't like you, either, but here we are. We'll get it annulled, but right now you have to go back to your room and change your clothes in a hurry. And I need to get dressed." When he started toward the door, she caught sight of his hand. "Wait! Take off Callan's ring."

"Right."

Anxiety knotted her stomach. "We *have* to tell them we got married."

"No, you were right the first time," he said grimly.

"This day is about them and there's no reason to distract from it with our bad decisions."

"We can't *not* tell them we got married with their rings." She twisted Molly's ring off her finger. "What kind of friend would I be if I let Molly get married with a *used* wedding ring? That has to be bad luck, right?"

"We only wore them for a few hours, and they certainly don't mean anything."

"Even more reason for them not to represent Molly and Callan's love for the rest of their lives. Leave me Callan's and I'll sneak away at some point and find new ones the same size. Then they'll never need to know." Her credit card would know. This trip hadn't been in her budget, but she rarely used her emergency card and she'd told herself she deserved it. Plus, she didn't want to disappoint Molly. But jewelry was pushing the limit—literally. "If they do notice, I'll say I lost them and didn't want to tell her. *And* you can pay me back for half the cost."

"Okay." He set the ring on top of the marriage certificate. "So we're agreed that nobody is ever going to find out about this."

"It's probably the first thing we've ever agreed on."

His mouth quirked up for a second. "Not the *first* thing, I guess."

Chelsea was still processing the fact he'd made a joke when he bent and picked up something off the floor near the foot of the bed. When he stood straight and tossed her phone onto the mattress near her, she winced and reached for it—careful not to let the covers slip. When she tapped the screen, the low battery warning popped up. She'd be lucky to get through breakfast before her phone was dead.

It took some doing, but she managed to snatch her charging cord and plug in the phone without flashing her breasts. She almost dropped the covers, though, when she saw the number of notifications her messaging, Facebook and Instagram apps were showing. To say there were *a lot* was an understatement.

Judging by the blistering streak of curses from John, his phone also still had juice. "Callan wants to know who served as my best man."

"Oh, no. No, no, no," Chelsea muttered as she opened the Facebook app and followed the notifications straight to the Perkin' Up Café's page.

She'd posted a photo of them in the chapel. She didn't know who had taken it, so maybe she'd asked somebody to take it with her phone. Or maybe one of them had paid for a photographer. With a wince, she added checking her credit card statement to her mental task list.

In the photograph, John had his arm around her waist and was bending her back slightly as he kissed her. He was wearing shorts and a short-sleeved button-down shirt in deference to the heat in Nevada, and she was wearing her sinfully red dress that hugged her curves, with strappy sandals that showed off the matching red polish on her toes. Her cloud of blond hair had started the night in a neat bun on top of her head, but by picture time, wisps of hair were escaping and she looked mussed. She was holding the bouquet in the air with one foot lifted, and even though their mouths were touching, they were both smiling. They looked like the happiest, most in love couple she'd ever seen.

Forget shots—no more tequila, period. Ever. Not even in a mixed drink.

How hot is my new husband? Happy wedding day to meeeeeee!!!

The caption would have made her laugh if the hot husband in question wasn't currently glaring at her as if this was all her fault.

Then she pulled up her Instagram account and found the same photo and caption, along with bonus hashtags.

#HotHusband #JustMarried #VegasBride #WeddingNightTime #NoBlushingForThisBride #UpAllNight #TequilaToastToTheBrideAndGroom #PerkinUpCafe #FletcherDigitalRestorationandDesign

Her headache got fifty percent worse.

"Hashtag no blushing for this bride?" John asked, giving her a look that made her want to pull the covers up over her head.

"I thought I blocked you from my Instagram because you're a jerk."

"I wouldn't know since I've never tried to see your Instagram, but Callan sent me a screenshot."

"I'm blocking him, too."

He snorted. "Too bad you didn't block everybody in Stonefield *before* you announced we got married and were...how did you put it? Oh, *up all night*."

"I hate you."

"And yet you told everybody you know how hot I am."

"Get out of my room." She threw a pillow at him—*his* pillow, she thought—but he easily ducked it, and he was laughing when he left.

Jerk.

Chapter Two

What's better than one Las Vegas wedding? TWO Las Vegas weddings! According to an announcement on the Perkin' Up Café's Facebook Page, not only did Chelsea Grey and John Fletcher accompany Molly Cyrs and Callan Avery for their wedding weekend, but they tied the knot themselves! Double congratulations to the happy couples!

—Stonefield Gazette *Facebook Page*

Of all the women in Las Vegas last night, John couldn't believe he'd woken up married to Chelsea Grey. He'd vowed to love and honor until death did they part the woman who'd done nothing but vex him since the day he moved to Stonefield.

And of course they hadn't stopped there. No, he'd had to wake up *naked* next to the cranky barista who was his business neighbor. Not that she was cranky with anybody else—she seemed to save her bad moods just for him.

It wasn't his fault she'd had to close for several days so her coffee shop could get an electrical upgrade. He'd been perfectly within his rights to complain to the landlord that his lights dimmed every time she ran one of her fancy coffee machines. And no, he didn't like coffee shop litter outside his office. Had she taken the complaints with grace?

No. She'd had his car towed for being slightly crooked and encroaching on one of the spots she'd talked the town into limiting to fifteen minutes so it was easier for her customers to find parking. Chelsea Grey was not a woman he even liked to share an aisle with in Dearborn's Market. And now he'd shared her bed.

No more tequila shots. Ever.

Once he was back in his room, he sent a reply to Callan's message asking him who had been his best man.

Tequila was my best man and I'm never speaking to him again. Will fill you in later, but have to shower and make it to the buffet on time.

Resigned to spending breakfast explaining to his friends what had happened—including the part where he woke up wearing Callan's wedding ring—he plugged his phone in and then took the fastest shower of his life. He was dressed and making sure he'd have everything he needed for a day of playing tourist when he realized he should have stayed in Chelsea's room until he could verify that she'd removed her drunken marriage announcements from all of her social media platforms.

Before unplugging his phone, he opened the Facebook app, and that was when he realized two things. First, based on his notifications, she'd tagged his business Page. Even though trying to click through told him she'd deleted the post, anybody who followed him might have seen it while it was still up. Second, the *Stonefield Gazette* had been right on top of sharing that fun bit of gossip on *their* Facebook Page, of course. But whoever ran that account hadn't simply shared Chelsea's post. They'd created their own post, which meant she couldn't delete it.

There was no way his brother and sister-in-law hadn't seen it, and they were never going to let him live this down—even when he'd moved on from Stonefield. After his divorce, John had realized how out of touch he was with Bruce, and with Ann-Marie and their daughters. He'd moved to Stonefield with the intention of staying a year, getting to know his nieces, and then he'd move on to a city—he didn't see himself as a small-town guy—close enough to visit regularly.

He couldn't imagine what they'd think when they read about his marriage—they might even get their hopes up he intended to stay in Stonefield. And since Bruce and Ann-Marie weren't unaware of the animosity between John and his new bride, they were probably confused.

What a mess. Shaking his head, he put the phone in his pocket and headed for the door. He wasn't sure if she'd been serious about blocking him on Instagram or not, but he didn't have time to look for her account. He'd just catch up with her and confirm she'd deleted that post, too. While there was nothing he could do to keep the news from spreading, he could at least make sure the ill-advised hashtags went away.

Up all night.

That had to be an exaggeration. A man didn't get so drunk he'd marry a woman he couldn't stand, and then make love all night. And she'd probably posted the pictures and written the captions before they got naked—maybe from the wedding chapel itself—so it was meant to be funny and not factually accurate.

By some stroke of luck—apparently the only one he was going to get this trip—John caught up with Chelsea outside the breakfast buffet and stopped her from entering with a hand on her arm.

She whirled, her green eyes going wide with alarm until she recognized him. He dropped his hand immediately, belatedly realizing he should have gotten her attention some other way. Her hair was in a ponytail now and dry, but she'd obviously sped through a shower because her skin still held the heat and moisture, and she smelled delicious.

And her face quickly settled into the expression she seemed to reserve just for him—unhappy to see him and highly annoyed at having to speak to him.

"I don't think we should go in together," she said as though it would be unusual for two people who knew each other and were going to the same place at the same time to have met up at the entrance.

"Our marriage made the Stonefield Gazette Facebook Page, so walking into a breakfast buffet together isn't going to shock anybody."

Her eyes narrowed. "Just because we're married now doesn't mean I want to spend any more time with you than I have to for Molly's sake."

"Ditto. I just wanted to make sure you deleted those posts."

"I did." Pink colored the tops of her cheeks. "*The Gazette* posted about it, though, and I can't delete that. And I can't bring myself to message them the truth, so I'm going to ignore it for now. Facing Molly and Callan is all I can handle right now."

Not giving the weekly newspaper the whole truth felt the right call. "Since we can't do anything about our marriage being Facebook official, we may as well go in and eat something."

She looked as if he'd just suggested they rob a casino. "How can you eat anything right now?"

"I need to eat because I drank a *lot* of alcohol last night and then…well, it seems that was followed by some strenuous physical activity, so I need food."

"I don't know about *strenuous*," she muttered.

"I remember strenuous."

She lifted a shoulder. "I remember an effort, at least."

John felt the heat spreading across his face. This woman infuriated him without even breaking a sweat. "I'm going to find Callan and Molly and then have some breakfast. Feel free to do whatever you think is best."

He started to walk away, but he didn't get far before Chelsea fell into step beside him. "You're right. I should eat. And this city isn't big enough for me to hide from Molly, so I might as well have a cinnamon roll while I face the music. I just hope she thinks it's funny and doesn't think I ruined the whole trip—and her wedding."

As annoying as he found her, he couldn't harden his heart against the anxiety in her voice. Worrying you've ruined the happiest day of a good friend's life was no small thing. He stopped walking and put his hand on her arm again.

Her skin was so soft.

Unbidden, a memory of running his hand down her back to cup the curve of her ass filled his mind and he shifted his weight from foot to foot. He couldn't stop random images from popping into his head, and as unlikely as it seemed, he found himself wishing he'd been sober enough to really remember the night.

"What?" she snapped, glaring at him.

He cleared his throat, thankful for the sharp reminder he didn't like this woman any more than she liked him—which was not at all. "You're not facing the music alone. *We* had too much to drink and did something impulsive and ill-advised. If anybody's going to find the humor in that, it's Molly. And if Molly's okay, Callan will be okay. We didn't ruin anything last night, and it will stay not ruined if we can all just accept it was stupid and laugh it off."

"You're right." The lines of her face softened as she relaxed.

"Maybe we could…lie a little, though," he added. "They don't need to know we had sex last night."

"It's not unrealistic that being drunk enough for the two of us to think marrying each other was a good idea would also mean being drunk enough to pass out as soon as we got back to my room."

"Exactly." He realized he was still touching her and dropped his hand. "So this was all a drunken lark misadventure that will make for a funny story someday. And someday is probably going to be today if I know Molly."

"Okay. Let's go eat."

It took them a few minutes to make their way to the table their friends had claimed, making them officially three minutes late. Considering the night they'd had, John didn't think that was too bad. Callan and Molly were deep in conversation as they approached, and judging by how animated Molly's expression and hands were, they were talking about the Facebook post.

Callan saw them first, and John felt a flood of

relief when it was obvious his friend was trying not to bust out laughing. As much as he hated being the butt of a joke, it was better than Callan being angry with him.

"Congratulations, Mr. and Mrs. Fletcher," Molly said, amusement dancing in her eyes. "Sleep well?"

Chelsea was *not* going to ruin Molly's wedding day by running upstairs to her room, grabbing her bags and getting on the first flight back to New Hampshire. She wanted to, but she wouldn't. She was going to act like the grown—and *married*, with a body still tingling from the aftermath of sex she couldn't remember—woman that she was and get through this breakfast.

"You know," Callan said, "I had faith you guys would at least pretend to get along this week for our sake, but I didn't expect this. Your dedication is next level."

"Tequila," Chelsea and John said at the same time.

"Look at all that marital harmony already," Molly said. "We got an extra pitcher of water because you're probably going to need it. We've got a full day today."

Chelsea barely managed to hold back the groan. Molly was hard to keep up with on a good day, and today was definitely not a good day. She just wanted to go back to bed—alone this time—and pull the covers up over her head.

"Coffee," she said, reaching for the carafe in the

middle of the table. "And John thinks coffee is disgusting, so dibs on his."

"Or you could divide it equally among the three of you," he said, probably just disagreeing with her out of habit. That was how contrary the man was.

She held up the carafe. "I guess since I'm your wife, what's yours is *mine*."

John almost choked on his water and for a second, Chelsea was afraid she was going to wear the mouthful of coffee Molly had just taken, but they both managed to swallow. She took advantage of the time it took Molly and Callan to stop laughing to pour herself a cup of coffee.

John didn't seem to find it funny, but she didn't care. All's fair in love, war and the pursuit of caffeine, she thought.

"Too soon," he said, and she was surprised he could talk with his jaw clenched like that. "Definitely too soon."

Callan pushed back his chair. "I'm hitting the buffet line and then I want to hear all the details."

Chelsea's appetite hadn't recovered from the previous night, but she forced herself to fill a plate. She'd eat what she could—slowly—because she needed fuel. She wasn't going to get through everything Molly had planned for the day with nothing in her stomach but coffee.

She wasn't even sure she could make the walk back to the elevator bank, never mind explore Las Vegas. Disappointing Molly wasn't an option, though, so all she could do was pray the zip line wasn't on her friend's agenda.

"Okay," Callan said when they were all seated again. "Time for details."

"Tequila." Chelsea and John said it at the same time again.

"Too much of it," John added.

Chelsea looked down at her plate because Molly was giving her a look that reeked of speculation and she was afraid her friend was going to ask the obvious next question. She did *not* want to talk about waking up naked next to John Fletcher.

She was definitely going to think about it later because having sex with the man was a puzzle that was missing a lot of pieces. But she didn't want to *talk* about it anytime soon, if ever, but she was afraid everybody at the table was thinking about it right now. And Molly didn't have the best filter when it came to conversation.

"So you woke up…" Molly let the words fade away as her eyebrow arched, as expected. "Married? Together?"

It was suddenly very clear that it would be almost impossible to tell the story without confessing how they'd started their day. But maybe they could distract from the same-bed situation with some jewelry theft. "I woke up wearing your ring."

Molly's eyes widened. "That's *my* ring you're wearing in the photos? I wondered if it was, but since we went with plain gold bands, I couldn't know for sure."

"We're going to buy new bands for you two today," John assured her.

"So you woke up wearing *my* band, then," Callan said, and Chelsea braced herself for the inevitable conclusion. "I'm glad we didn't have them inscribed."

Before Chelsea could breathe a sigh of relief— thank goodness for Callan's practical mind—Molly spoke up. "But were you *together* when you woke up wearing our wedding rings?"

"These are surprisingly good scrambled eggs for a buffet," John said, and Chelsea rolled her eyes. She wasn't sure if he was trying to change the subject or if he was genuinely impressed, but either way, it was an odd thing to say.

"Did you try the home fries?" Callan pointed his fork at his plate. "They're pretty good, too."

Fortunately, Molly was willing to let it go—*for now*, her look promised. "You should wear the rings today and take a picture of your marriage certificate. Some places might have discounts or perks for newlyweds, you know."

They were both shaking their heads, but it was John who spoke. "Wearing a wedding ring to save on stuff when you're not married doesn't sit right."

"But you *are* married," Callan pointed out. "And who doesn't love a discount?"

John looked like he wanted to argue the point, but then his jaw tightened and he stabbed his fork into a chunk of cantaloupe. He probably knew, as Chelsea did, that a lot of ideas came out of Molly's mouth, but if Callan backed her up, it was a done deal. They'd be wearing their wedding bands today, probably as punishment for having used them in the first place.

"We won't be married for long," John insisted. "We're filing for an annulment immediately."

"Not today! Today is *my* wedding day," Molly said. "And I think it's bad luck to talk about annulments and divorce, so you can't even *talk* about it until tomorrow."

"Molly—" Chelsea began, because she was really pushing it now.

"Nope. No negativity on my wedding day." And that was that, because she was the bride.

When they were finished what little food they could fit in with all the water Molly made them drink, Chelsea stood. "I need a few minutes before we leave. I have to take something for my headache and—"

"And get your ring," Molly finished, even though it definitely wasn't what Chelsea had been about to say. "I'll go with you. Callan, you and John can hang out and I'll text you when we're on our way down."

Chelsea didn't bother arguing. It wouldn't do any good, so she led the way back to the elevators. To her friend's credit, Molly waited until they reached Chelsea's room and were behind the closed door before asking the question that had probably been bubbling up inside since she saw the worst social media posts ever.

"So how was the wedding night?" Molly actually winked. "If you know what I mean."

Of course Chelsea knew what she meant. Molly was many things, but subtle wasn't one of them. "Honestly, I don't remember much of last night."

"Considering you and John pretty much hate each other and then vowed to love each other forever, that doesn't surprise me. Your bar bill must have been astronomical, though."

Chelsea winced. "It probably didn't take that much," she said. "I don't drink very often and I suspect both of us are lightweights."

"So it's a mystery." Molly cocked her head. "Or a puzzle, and we just need to put the pieces together."

Chelsea groaned. She wasn't sure if it was related to Molly's ADHD, but if there was a puzzle, her friend was compelled to solve it. "*Or*, we can pretend it didn't happen and spend the day celebrating the fact you're getting married tonight. On purpose, without alcohol involved."

"Well, not a lot, anyway. Was John in your bed when you woke up?" Molly asked. Chelsea's cheeks flamed. "Well, that's a yes. Were you naked?"

Chelsea sighed and pressed her lips together.

"Okay, was *he* naked?"

Chelsea refused to answer. But even though she would have guessed it wasn't possible, her face felt even hotter.

"That wasn't much of a puzzle," Molly said. "So basically, the only thing we *don't* know is if he was any good."

Beneath the shock and horror of the morning—to

say nothing of the headache—her body had a lan-
guid, sated feeling she hadn't felt in a while, but still
recognized. While she couldn't say with any certainty John had been particularly good in bed, he'd
definitely gotten the job done.

"Maybe you can find out tonight."

Molly's words jerked Chelsea away from her
thoughts. "What?"

"What happens in Vegas stays in Vegas." Molly
shrugged. "Unless you post it on Instagram and your
Facebook Page, I guess."

"You're not funny."

She grinned. "I think my sense of humor's pretty
on point, considering you stole my wedding ring the
night before my wedding."

There was nothing but humor in her tone, but Chelsea still winced. It was going to be a very long time
before she didn't feel guilty about the rings. "Okay,
you're a little bit funny."

"Good. Let's go have some adventures. And remember, absolutely no talk about the A-word today.
I don't want that in the universe on the day I get married. Smile, act like happy newlyweds and try to score
some perks."

Sure, because the only thing more fun than waking up hungover and married to a total jerk in Las
Vegas was pretending to be happy about it.

Chapter Three

A permit has been issued for a children's birthday party to be hosted at the gazebo this afternoon, which means a dozen or more kids who've had a lot of sugar will be running amok in the town square. Please drive with extra caution between the hours of one and three o'clock. It's going to be on the chilly side, so dress warm, partygoers, and happy fourth birthday to Hunter!

—Stonefield Gazette *Facebook Page*

John lingered at the table for a few minutes after the women left, dragging out the time it took him to finish the last few swallows of juice and fold his napkin.

He wanted them to get enough of a head start so there was no chance he'd end up in an elevator with them.

His headache was abating slightly, unless he thought about Chelsea or the fact he'd married her last night. Then it flared up again.

"We should go upstairs and get that ring," Callan said, and then he pressed his lips together to keep from grinning.

"Chelsea has both of them. I forgot to put my stuff in the safe, though, so I still want to go up. I just don't want to run into them in the hall." When Callan chuckled, John shook his head. "You're enjoying this."

"Maybe a little. If I'd had to put odds on you getting drunk and ending up in a Vegas wedding chapel, I'd say…crap. I don't know anything about betting odds. Is a hundred to one good or bad?"

"Remind me to keep you away from the bookies. How long do you think they'll be?"

"Depends on how interesting the story gets *after* the wedding, probably," Callan said, and John groaned.

When they got into the elevator, he went straight to the back of the car and leaned his head against the wall, closing his eyes. He needed silence and darkness for a while, neither of which he was going to find in this city, it seemed. He hadn't even wanted to come, but he couldn't bring himself to let Callan down.

When John had finally opened his office about two and a half months ago, Callan had been one of the first residents of Stonefield to inquire about his services. While digital design for corporations paid his bills, digital restoration of old or damaged photographs was his passion. The library had a collection of extremely old town photographs that needed to be saved, but Callan didn't have a lot of room in his budget.

Because there was no timeline for completion and because John *wanted* to restore the pictures, he told Callan he'd do the first batch for a fraction of the cost. It would be a nice addition to his portfolio and give him some visibility. After a few meetings, the friendship had been cemented. Callan's oldest friend, who lived in New York City, hadn't been able to get away and that was how John had come to fly all the way across the country to be his best man.

And he'd known when he agreed that Chelsea was accompanying Molly to be her maid of honor. Her presence made the trip about ninety-eight percent less appealing, but he'd told himself he could be coolly polite to anybody for one weekend.

There was no way he could have guessed coolly polite plus tequila would equal waking up married to her.

Since it seemed like the elevator stopped on every floor, John didn't open his eyes until Callan nudged him. "This is your floor."

They had to walk by Chelsea's room to get to his, and John didn't allow himself to glance at her door. He definitely didn't allow himself to stop and press his ear to the door to see if he could hear their conversation. Chelsea had agreed they'd claim they passed out as soon as they got back to her room last night, but he was afraid once she and Molly were alone, she was going to forget that part of their conversation.

"Okay, what the hell happened?" Callan asked once they were in John's room. "I mean, I get that there was tequila involved, but based on the history between you two, I would have bet you'd be in the emergency room getting your stomach pumped before you drank enough tequila to put Molly's ring on her finger."

"We've already established you should never bet, but you're not wrong. Chelsea Grey would be my last choice for a wife."

Even as he said the words, an image flashed in his mind of Chelsea putting the ring on his finger.

"With this ring, I thee wed," she'd recited, and because he'd been drowning in tequila and her green eyes, he'd thought they were the most beautiful words he'd ever heard.

"Molly's punishing us, isn't she? By making us wear the rings all day?"

Callan shrugged. "It's hard to say. My guess is that it's a little bit punishment, but mostly that she finds it funny and also genuinely thinks there might be some newlywed perks to be scored. She wouldn't do it to be mean, though. If it upsets you, just say so."

John wasn't sure if *upset* was the right word. It bothered him. The ring would feel strange and conspicuous on his finger, and it would be a constant reminder of the huge mistake he'd made last night. But it would probably be more annoying than actually upsetting.

He shook his head. "Trying to score some discounts seems like the least we can do after getting drunk and stealing your wedding rings."

"Molly's going to get so much mileage out of this story, she probably doesn't even care."

John winced. Stonefield talking about him because he was helping restore the historic photos in their town archive was good. Talking about him because he'd had too many tequila shots and married the coffee shop owner—who the entire town knew he was in a low-key feud with—was *not* good.

"Maybe somebody will throw a punch at the budget committee meeting or something and everybody will forget about us."

Callan laughed. "Are you kidding? Everybody knows you two couldn't stand each other. And then those Facebook and Instagram posts? Stonefield's going to be talking about this for a very long time."

A phone chimed, and Callan slid his out of his pocket. He read a text message, chuckled, typed a response and then slid the phone back in his pocket without saying anything.

"Was that Molly?" John asked. "What did she say?"

"They're ready," he said. "And the rest is covered by spousal privilege."

"I think that's only in a court of law."

"Speaking of the law, Molly wasn't kidding when she said no talking about annulments today. She doesn't want to bring bad luck down on us."

"Can my luck *get* any worse?"

Callan chuckled and slapped his shoulder. "I don't know. Did you use a condom?"

Chelsea blinked as she stepped outside the hotel and the intense sunlight pierced her brain. She should have stopped in the gift shop and bought a pair of cheap sunglasses.

Unfortunately, nothing in this city seemed to be cheap. She'd made the decision to dust off her credit card for the trip so she could be here for Molly, and because she deserved a vacation, but she needed to make every penny count. And that was before she threw a hefty bar bill and a legal predicament into the mix, to say nothing of buying wedding bands. She'd just blink and hope the headache medicine kicked in soon.

"The car should be here any minute," Molly told them without looking up from her phone.

Her friend had assured them all several times that she'd researched Uber and would be able to get them cars to go wherever they needed to. It wasn't a service they had in Stonefield, so Chelsea was skeptical. But Callan had moved to their little town from New York City, and he *had* to be pretty proficient with the app. When she'd started to point that out, he'd shaken his head and pulled her aside. Molly was very excited about checking Uber off her travel bucket list and he didn't want to ruin it for her. But yes, in a bind, he'd get them a car.

When her phone buzzed in her hand, she assumed it was Molly, probably wanting to add to their conversation upstairs without the guys hearing. But the preview on her lock screen showed the entire text message and it was from a contact named "Hubby."

Did we use a condom?

Chelsea almost dropped her phone, and in the process of fumbling it, she got Molly's attention. She managed to hit the button to lock the screen before her friend could see it.

Hubby? She had no memory of adding John to her contacts, or giving him her number.

And as to his question, *that* possible nightmare hadn't even occurred to her. Her knees trembled slightly, as did the smile she gave Molly—who was frowning at her—and she forced herself to take a deep breath.

And then she remembered laughing while he fumbled with a condom wrapper. Something about Callan giving him a box and telling him to have one in his pocket at all times because with all the women in Vegas, John was sure to find one who liked grumpy computer nerds.

Because she didn't want to attract Molly's attention again, she caught John's eye and gave one short nod. His visible relief would have been funny under other circumstances.

Then she noticed Callan typing on *his* phone and a few seconds later, Molly's phone buzzed. Because of the way they were standing, Chelsea could read the preview on her screen.

She's in his phone as "Wifey."

Molly laughed before swiping away the text so she could continue stalking their Uber, while Chelsea pressed her hands to her cheeks in a futile attempt to hide the blush. Then she stepped backward into the shade of the tall building as Molly and Callan started talking to a man trying to give them a flyer.

John took the opportunity their distraction offered and joined her in the shade. "Did you have to change your name in my contacts to *Wifey*?"

She hated when he used that stern, judgmental tone, and since it seemed to be the only tone he used with *her*, she pretty much hated the sound of his voice. "How do you know I did it? Maybe *you* changed it to *Wifey* before you put yourself in my phone as *Hubby*."

"That definitely wasn't me. I wouldn't do that."

"Says the guy who woke up naked in my bed with Callan's wedding ring on his finger." She didn't bother to soften the snarky edge to her voice. She could do a *tone*, too. His jaw clenched and he didn't respond. "And I noticed you said my contact name was *changed*, which means I was already in your phone. You certainly weren't in mine."

"The Perkin' Up Café was in my contacts because our landlord wanted me to be able to reach you directly after the second time you almost knocked out our power and that time you set the fire alarms off. Apparently, you use your cell for your business number, as I do," he said. "Your business shares a wall with mine and you have a lot of heating elements drawing electricity. There's a high potential for a problem over there, so knowing how to reach you is common sense."

"I burned *one* bagel." She rolled her eyes. "And I'm brewing coffee, not running space heaters off extension cords."

"One never knows with you."

Chelsea's hands curled into fists, which she rested on her hips. The man really was one of the most pompous asses she'd ever met. But before she could tell him what she really thought of him, Molly moved into her line of vision.

"Hey, newlyweds," her friend said in a bright voice, and Chelsea heard John's low growl. "The car's here."

It was a minivan, and of course she ended up with John in the third-row seat. She would have preferred to have Molly with her and the guys could have the middle row, but since they were here for Molly and Callan's wedding, she kept her mouth shut. Luckily, there was enough space between them so John's legs didn't touch hers.

"Next stop, the Eiffel Tower!" Molly said as she buckled her seat belt, her excitement evident. She leaned forward slightly so she could talk to the driver. "We're getting married tonight. And our friends in the backseat got married last night."

John growled again, and she thought she heard Callan snicker before Molly elbowed him.

"Congratulations," the driver said, and Chelsea admired the way he seemed genuinely happy for them despite the fact he probably heard something like it multiple times per day.

"Is she going to tell everybody we see?" John muttered, not quite as under his breath as he thought, because Molly twisted in her seat to look at him.

"Probably not everybody," she said. "But I'll definitely tell whoever sells us wedding rings to replace the ones you two used to get married."

Chelsea glanced sideways in time to see the guilty flush color John's cheeks and she enjoyed that, even though she was as guilty as he was. Then Molly laughed, and Callan joined in. After a few seconds, John chuckled.

Then he looked at Chelsea and shook his head. "We're never going to live this down, are we?"

She gave him a tight smile. "No. Never."

Chapter Four

Chief Bordeaux would like to remind every-body that decaying pumpkins are not only unattractive, but they also attract nuisance animals. If your Jack-o'-lantern looks like it's melting, it's time to discard it properly. (Prop-erly does not mean smashing it in the street, throwing it at passing vehicles, or tossing it over the fence into your neighbor's yard.)
—Stonefield Gazette *Facebook Page*

John's feet hurt. His back was starting to hurt. And his headache, though mostly gone, was still making its presence felt now and then. He'd drunk so much water, his back teeth were floating and he'd spent more time than he cared to think about touring the public restrooms of Las Vegas.

Now they were in their fourth Uber of the day, and he was once again sitting next to Chelsea. This vehicle was a little smaller, and their elbows kept bumping. Each time, she would jerk away, trying to lean the other way. Tense silence and a low hum of hostility stretched between them, and he tried to ignore the sizzle of remembered chemistry that kept bubbling up from his subconscious.

He'd tuned out Molly's excited chatter, trying to think of something to say to Chelsea—some inane bit of small talk to break the ice that had reformed between them. They hadn't spoken to each other at all for at least an hour—since the four of them left a jewelry store where he and Chelsea had each charged a new gold band. Thankfully, their friends had simple taste in jewelry, but it still hurt. He'd pointed to a sign that said they'd accept gold in trade, but Callan had shaken his head before tipping it toward Molly, who was looking at outrageously expensive watches.

Chelsea hadn't spoken to him since. And nothing came to him that he could be sure wouldn't set her off and escalate the hostility. They just didn't have anything to talk about, but the closer they got to ceremony time, the more he felt compelled to try.

He and Chelsea weren't the first couple to get drunk and get married in Las Vegas, and they wouldn't be the last. The fault was shared, and it was a mistake they'd rectify. There was no sense in ruining their trip.

"Molly, I hate to break it to you," Chelsea said, the sound of her voice dragging him out of his thoughts and back into the conversation around him. "But I don't think it's possible to see the entire city of Las Vegas in one day."

"Not with that attitude, it's not," Molly responded, and their driver tried and failed to disguise a bark of laughter as a cough. "But we're almost done. We're going to visit Fremont Street for a couple hours, and then we're going back to the hotel."

A couple hours. When he did finally make it back to his room, he was going to have to avoid lying down on—or maybe even sitting on—the bed or he might sleep through the ceremony. And *that* Molly wouldn't forgive him for.

She'd already forgiven them for the rings. They'd found gold bands she liked even more than the ones John and Chelsea were wearing—even though John couldn't see a difference—and having been bought in Las Vegas made them even more special to her. Or so she claimed.

And he did appreciate that they'd gotten a few discounts and perks thanks to their rings and the marriage certificate. The free dessert after they ate lunch was especially appreciated.

Fremont Street was a lot, though. It was lights and noise and crowds, and his introverted nature was ready to crawl into a blanket fort. After a half hour, he was really starting to lag behind and Chelsea finally spoke to him.

"Vegas isn't a great place to nurse a hangover," she said, looking at him with concern. "Is your headache any better?"

"Yeah, it's not bad. This isn't really my thing, though," he said. "I wouldn't have minded a tour of the local library."

Chelsea laughed, and he had to admit she had a really great laugh. "You could have talked Callan into that, but Molly's far too wound up to take in a quiet environment."

"Yeah. I don't know how he's keeping up with her, even without a hangover." They were already so far ahead he could barely see them. But he heard her call for Chelsea, probably to show her something. "You should hurry. I'll catch up."

"If you ditch us, Molly will find you and you'll be sorry."

He chuckled. "Don't tempt me."

John took his time on the catching-up part. Molly had Chelsea, and Callan would understand him hanging back for a little bit. He'd found a relatively quiet area and he was perusing some souvenirs—more for the quiet than for a desire for a neon-flashing ball cap—when his phone rang.

His brother's name flashed on the screen and John's thumb hovered over the decline button. He had no idea how he was going to explain this mess to his brother, and it was all too much for the phone.

But he'd already known Bruce would have seen the posts—or Ann-Marie would have and then shown him, more likely—and he couldn't leave him hanging. He was surprised he'd waited this long to call. John stepped away from the vendor table and accepted the call. "Hey."

"What the hell?"

"Right?"

"You're on speakerphone, by the way," Bruce said, and John pinched the bridge of his nose. Of course his sister-in-law wasn't going to be left out of this conversation.

"Hi, John," Ann-Marie said. "What the hell?"

"Where are the girls?" He loved talking to his nieces, but this probably wasn't a good conversation for them to eavesdrop on.

"They're outside," Ann-Marie said. "Spill."

"There's a lot going on here, so the short version is too much tequila."

Bruce snorted. "You're in a city full of beautiful women and you marry the one who had your car towed? How much tequila did you drink?"

"All of it, I think. That was last night and I'm not one hundred percent sure I could pass a field sobriety test right now."

"I thought they wouldn't marry you if you were visibly under the influence," Ann-Marie said.

"Either Chelsea and I are incredibly good actors or we found an officiant who didn't care."

Bruce made a low whistling sound. "You don't remember?"

"It's all pretty blurry."

"Speaking of tequila, did you—" A grunting sound cut off his brother's words, probably due to his sister-in-law running interference.

"I thought it was a joke," Ann-Marie said. "Like a prank."

"Unfortunately, we have the paperwork to prove otherwise."

"Have you called Mom yet?" Bruce asked, and with him it was hard to tell if he was joking or not.

"I'm not telling Mom. You don't remember all the crying when I told her Pam and I split up?"

"You can't *not* tell Mom you got married."

"It's not a real marriage." He cleared his throat. "Okay, it's real, but it's temporary. We're filing for annulment as soon as we get home, which will mean it never happened. There's no reason to tell her."

What would he even say? *Hey, remember that woman I ranted about for a full ten minutes after I moved here? Well, thanks to poor choices regarding tequila, she's your new daughter-in-law.*

"She doesn't need to know," he said again, more firmly this time. "And I need to go. Molly's got us running all over this damn city, trying to see everything in one day."

"That's fun with a hangover." Bruce didn't even try to hide his amusement.

"I'm hanging up now," John said, and then he did.

Knowing the conversation was just a preview of what he could expect when they got home didn't improve his mood any. Sure, they'd screwed up in a colossal way, but if Chelsea hadn't announced it to the entire world, nobody would have known. They could have cleaned up the mess privately and put it behind them.

But when he spotted Callan in the crowd and then heard the women's voices, he wiped the scowl off his face and put the phone call out of his mind. This was going to be a joyful day for his friends, no matter how hard he had to pretend.

"We're going to cut this short and head back," Callan said, putting his arm around Molly's shoulders. "The overstimulation's starting to kick in."

That was when John realized Molly had been crying, and she was a little pale. She jerked away from Callan and crossed her arms. "I'm fine."

He'd been friends with the couple long enough to know when Molly was cranky, it usually stemmed from her ADHD. And once she started spinning, it was hard to pull her out of it.

"Well, I'm not fine," he said with a chuckle. He had to think fast, coming up with a valid reason to bail on her plan. "For somebody who sits at a desk all day, every day, this was a lot of walking and I'm beat. And I think I have blisters forming on my feet."

As expected, Molly's instant concern for him distracted her and short-circuited the part of her brain that was working up a temper. "Ouch. Those don't look like new shoes."

"They're not, but walking around Dearborn's Market and walking around Las Vegas aren't quite the same," he said, and they all laughed.

"If we head back now, we can spend extra time on hair and makeup," Chelsea said. "Maybe we can do facials since we've been sweating all day."

"Yes!" Molly bounced on the balls of her feet, and John wondered where she got her sudden bursts of energy from. He had no bounce in him at all. "Let me call another Uber."

When Molly and Callan turned their attention to her phone, Chelsea stepped closer to John and put her hand on his arm. Every nerve in his body seemed to zero in on that contact as she leaned in to speak quietly.

"That was really nice. She's definitely done."

He looked into her eyes and the usual surge of annoyance didn't come. "Contrary to our past interactions, I'm not a bad guy if you take the time to get to know me."

"I guess I'm getting to know you pretty well now," she said, and then she laughed.

John didn't find that particularly funny, but she didn't notice because the simple sound of her laughter triggered a smile he couldn't hold back.

Chapter Five

According to our librarian, Mr. Callan Avery,
the Books & Brews book club will still meet
this coming Wednesday at Sutton's Place Brew-
ery & Tavern. There was some question if he
and his new bride will be back from Las Vegas
in time, but he assures us he'll be there with
his reader questions in hand. And he left a
few copies with Irish Sutton at the taproom if
you're a fast reader and want to join in the fun!
　　　　　—Stonefield Gazette *Facebook Page*

The plan was to meet in the sitting area near the elevator bank on their floor and then all go down together. They'd briefly considered trying to meet at
the wedding chapel—thankfully not the same one

John and Chelsea had ended up at, which would have been too awkward for words—so the groom wouldn't see the bride before the ceremony, but that plan got complicated fast and they scrapped it.

Chelsea gave Molly a final looking over, but there was nothing more she could do. Her friend had achieved peak bridal perfection.

Molly's dress was in her favorite retro style, with a fitted sleeveless bodice and a flared skirt that hit below her knee. Her dark hair was pulled back in a long ponytail. In lieu of a veil, she had a length of white tulle tied around the ponytail, with white sequins sparkling in the trailing ends. With pearls in her ears and at her throat, and with slightly more dramatic makeup than usual, she was so beautiful, tears welled up in Chelsea's eyes.

"No crying!" Molly flapped her hands in front of Chelsea's face as if that would dry her eyes. "You'll make me cry and our mascara will run and we'll look like raccoons in my wedding photos. Exceptionally pretty raccoons, but still."

Chelsea laughed. "Like I didn't use waterproof mascara? Honey, that stuff's so waterproof, we'll probably still have full lashes next week."

Molly laughed, and then stepped back to look Chelsea up and down. "I was so right about your dress, too. It looks so pretty on you."

Chelsea faced the mirror, smoothing the pink fabric. The knee-length gown had three-quarter sleeves and hugged her curves. It wasn't her style or color because she usually wore bolder gem tones—like the red dress she wore last night to her *own* wedding, she thought with a wince—but it was really lovely. Her hair was also in a ponytail, though it was thicker and not as long as Molly's.

Chelsea's phone chimed and she had to work at getting it out of the small wristlet that matched her dress. She'd bought it not thinking about the fact she might have Molly's phone, too. "Your husband-to-be wants to know if you're still marrying him or if you got cold feet and climbed down the fire escape."

"Of course I'm still—wait, *is* there a fire escape? It can't be a ladder this high up, can it? Do the windows even open?"

Chelsea caught Molly's wrist when she started heading toward the window. "You can tumble down that research rabbit hole later. Right now it's time for you to go get married."

The second they turned the corner to where the guys were waiting, Chelsea realized she'd forgotten to take the wedding band off her finger. And John's gaze only flickered over Molly before landing on her, so there was no way to take it off and tuck it in the wristlet without drawing more attention to it.

And, *wow*, John Fletcher looked hot as hell in a suit.

Both men were in gray, with the groom's a slightly darker shade. And both men looked good. But John filled his out in a way that made her forget she didn't like him and had her fingernails leaving indentations in the palms of her hands.

His eyebrow arched, and one corner of his mouth tilted up. He might be trying to look smug, but she'd seen the flare of heat in his eyes when he saw her.

She probably shouldn't even be in the same room as tequila tonight.

They were quiet as they rode down in the elevator and went out to wait for their Uber. Callan couldn't stop smiling, and Molly was practically vibrating with excitement. It was a smaller vehicle this time, and the entire side of Chelsea's body, from shoulder to knee, was pressed against John. Strangely, she didn't mind as much as she'd thought.

"Make sure the videographer is good," Molly whispered as they walked into the chapel. "My mom's going to want to see everything."

"I'm on it," Chelsea said.

"And make sure they get some good shots of Elvis."

"I will."

She felt a hand on her back and she realized it was John's. He leaned close. "Wait, she's really doing the Elvis thing?"

"Of course she is." She hung back as Molly and Callan stepped forward to speak with a man who was probably Elvis's assistant. Or manager.

"We should ask him about annulments while we're here," John whispered.

"We can't," she whispered back. "We promised her we wouldn't talk about it today."

"What are you two whispering about?" Molly demanded, making Chelsea jump.

"What a gorgeous bride you are," John said without missing a beat.

When Molly beamed and then turned back to the assistant/manager, Chelsea gave John a sideways look. "You're good at coming up with on-the-spot lies."

"Thank you, I think. I'm not sure if that's a compliment or not."

"Take it however you want."

His eyebrow arched, but a smile tugged at the corners of his lips. "Really?"

Chelsea rolled her eyes, but turned away before he could see the blush heating her cheeks, really hoping she'd imagined the innuendo. Spending the day with John had shown her a different side of him—he really was kind to Molly—and maybe she didn't dislike him as much as she had before the tequila. Him flirting with her, though? That would mess with her head.

"It's time," Molly exclaimed, jerking Chelsea out of her conflicted thoughts.

After a very quick check-in with the still photographer and videographer they'd added to the wedding package, Chelsea took her place by Molly. John took his place next to Callan, and Elvis cleared his throat.

Chelsea mostly paid attention. It was hard, though, with John in her sightline, looking unusually hot in that suit. She fiddled with the ring on her finger, twisting the gold band, until she caught John looking at her hand.

She turned her body slightly, forcing her attention to Molly and Callan. They both looked so happy as the Elvis impersonator led them through their vows, she couldn't help getting teary eyed. This was such a Molly thing to do, and though she knew Paul and Amanda Cyrs weren't very happy about it, she was glad Callan had made this happen for her.

They'd have a reception back in Stonefield at some point, of course. And Molly had already said she'd wear her mother's dress when that happened. But this was the ceremony of Molly's heart and Chelsea was honored to be here for it.

The part where she ended up with a husband of her own wasn't great, but they'd fix that.

Once the deed was done and the papers were signed, they piled into the limo that had been a pricey addition to the wedding package. After a few stops to take photos at some of the most famous landmarks, the driver delivered them back to their hotel, where they had a dinner reservation.

Too much prime rib, a few champagne toasts and an amazing slice of wedding cake later, Chelsea was exhausted. How they all managed to laugh so hard when they were so full, she wasn't sure, but they did. They'd laughed so much her stomach hurt and it wasn't just the champagne. The joy of the evening had dulled the animosity arcing between her and John, and she had to admit they made a great foursome when the two of them could get along.

"It's time for this bride and her groom to make our grand exit," Molly said after stifling a yawn.

"I should have saved some of my rice pilaf to throw at you," John said, and Chelsea choked down a laugh. He was a funny guy when he wasn't being a jerk.

Molly hugged her while Callan shook John's hand, and then they left—holding hands while the bride practically skipped alongside her new husband. Meanwhile, Chelsea was left in awkward silence with *her* husband. And neither of them could get up and walk away because they needed their server to stop by with the check so they could have it split between the two of them. Another charge she couldn't really afford, but they weren't about to let the bride and groom pay.

She managed to avoid making eye contact with John by fiddling with the stuff on the table. After stacking her cake plate with Molly's, she rested their forks across the top. Then she gathered the water glasses together.

She was down to picking crumbs off the tablecloth when the server finally appeared. He didn't have the check with him, though.

"Will you be having after-dinner cocktails?" he asked.

"No," Chelsea and John said at the same time.

It was probably going to be a while before John touched hard liquor again. And he certainly wasn't going to have cocktails while alone with Chelsea

Grey. Not after the champagne he'd already con-
sumed.

Having a chaperone on hand now couldn't make
them go back in time, pass on the tequila and skip
saying *I do*, but having somebody watching him
in this moment would help him ignore the interest
he had in his new wife. Rather than fading away
with his hangover, his inability to put her out of his
mind—or to keep his eyes off her—was inexplica-
bly growing stronger.

She looked beautiful tonight. Not as stunning as
she had last night in the red dress—her *wedding
dress*, he thought wryly—but the pink dress hugged
her curves and made his hands itch to follow them.

Finishing off the glass of water he'd been nursing
instead of adding more champagne to his blood alcohol content did nothing to cool him off, and he knew
he needed to get back upstairs. He'd lock himself in
his room, take a shower and turn the television on to
some mind-numbingly boring show to fall asleep to.

"I guess I'll turn in," Chelsea said, picking up the
little bag she'd set on the table.

Manners had him on his feet before his brain
could tell him to stay seated, and he moved quickly
to pull out her chair as she stood. That put him a lot
closer to her than he should be, of course, and when
she was on her feet, he held his breath so he wouldn't
lean in and inhale the scent of her hair. There was
something about being close to her that made him
forget what a pain in the butt she was.

"Thank you," she said, and there was a slight tremor in her voice.

John knew he should let her walk away. The best thing for him right now was to not be able to see her and definitely to have her out of arm's reach. But there were thousands of people in the hotel and he wasn't comfortable with her being alone in the elevator and hallways.

"I'll walk you to your room," he said, and he was rewarded with a withering glare. "For safety reasons. Once you've locked your door, I'll go to my room and lock myself in."

"Okay, for safety reasons."

When they started walking, he almost put his hand on the small of her back to guide her around a group of people, and he had to shove it into the pocket of his pants instead. His inability to stop thinking about touching this woman irritated him, and it came out in his voice. "Champagne's not as potent as tequila, thankfully."

She gave him a look that bordered on offended before her lips twisted into a humorless smile. "Thank goodness for that."

They didn't speak again. They waited for an elevator and then stood side by side while it stopped at ten different floors before reaching theirs. He stood back to let her go first and her arm brushed his stomach. Sucking in a breath, he hoped she wouldn't notice the way he flinched.

He stood quietly while she got her key card out of

her bag and unlocked the door. Maybe under other circumstances, he would have gone in and turned the lights on for her and checked the closet and shower for unwelcome guests, but if he crossed that threshold, he was afraid he wouldn't come out until morning. Vegas had to be magical, he thought, because the chemistry between them was stronger than their mutual dislike. They'd already learned that the hard way, but they didn't need to make it worse.

When she had the door open, he put his foot against it to hold it open. "I'll wait while you turn the lights on."

She chuckled, but she turned the lights on and then checked the bathroom and closet before coming back to the door. "No bad guys. Thank you for walking back with me."

He nodded and withdrew his foot. "Good night, Chelsea."

"Good night."

Once he heard the security bar locking into place, John walked the rest of the way to his room. After stripping out of the suit and pulling on sleep pants, he grabbed a bottle of water from the mini-fridge— screw the cost—and stood at the window, looking out over the bright lights of the city.

Then his gaze slid to the wedding band on the desk and he sighed. *What a weekend this has been*, he thought.

And then he wondered if he should have offered to unzip Chelsea's dress. Maybe just the feel of his knuckles grazing the smooth skin of her back would have been enough to take the edge off so he could sleep.

He actually laughed out loud at himself. That wasn't what would have happened at all if he'd unzipped that pink dress.

It was tempting to call Bruce. His brother's practicality came in handy sometimes. He was a very common-sense guy and even though he liked to give John a hard time, there was nobody better for helping him get his head on straight.

But there was the time difference. Bruce and Ann-Marie would be asleep, and John's needing a verbal cold shower wouldn't be a good reason to wake them up in his sister-in-law's book. Either that or they'd remind him what happened in Vegas stayed in Vegas and tell him to go for it.

But what happened in Vegas didn't always stay in Vegas, he reminded himself as he picked up the gold band. Tomorrow John was going back to Stonefield with a wife he'd vowed to love, honor and cherish for the rest of his life.

Chapter Six

News from the Stonefield Fire Department: The crew battled a fire on Poplar Road today. Thanks to a call from an observant passerby who spied smoke, the damage to the house was limited, but it will be uninhabitable until repairs are completed. The resident was not home at the time and no injuries were reported. It's believed the fire originated when dried leaves on the porch were ignited by a carelessly tossed cigarette, which in turn ignited empty boxes intended for recycling. Anybody with information about the incident should contact Chief Nelson at the fire department.
—Stonefield Gazette *Facebook Page*

Chelsea reached up, trying for the fifth or six time to adjust the overhead nozzle that, in theory, was blowing cool air over her. Planes always felt stuffy and overheated to her, but every time John's arm brushed hers or the length of his thigh rested against hers, the temperature crept up a few more degrees.

It was now approximately three hundred degrees on the plane.

When they boarded, a lot of the seats were already full. Callan and Molly were able to sit together, but Chelsea had to choose between sitting next to a harried woman with an infant, a guy in a business suit who'd actually looked her up and down before patting the seat next to him, or John.

She should have chosen the baby.

Chelsea had thrown a long, lightweight cardigan over a tank top and leggings for the flight because comfort always trumped fashion when traveling was involved. Now that she was overheating, she'd like to take the cardigan off, but it would be a struggle in the tight space.

"Are you okay?" John asked, and she heard annoyance rather than concern.

"I'm fine."

"You haven't been still since the plane took off. It's like sitting next to a toddler who had too much sugar."

"Do you actually hear the stuff that comes out of your mouth?" She rolled her eyes when he gave her a questioning look. "I can't tell if you just have an abrasive personality in general or if you reserve your insults for me."

"I've never been accused of being abrasive before," he said, and then shrugged. It was a non-answer that more or less let her know it was just her. "And it's not meant to be insulting. I'm simply describing my experience."

"No, you called me a hyperactive toddler."

"Fine," he snapped. "I apologize."

Rather than feeling mollified, Chelsea grew more annoyed and she actually welcomed the feeling. Bickering with John kept her from thinking about Friday night. Some of the memories weren't as fuzzy as they had been at first, and her mind kept wanting to poke at them like a tongue poking at a sore tooth.

It was a lot easier to remember she didn't like this guy if they were arguing than if she was reliving the feel of his mouth on her breast and his hand fisted in her hair.

"One of us has to be the one to file," she said, the words coming out of her in a rush in an effort to shove those memories out of her mind.

He gave her a sideways look. "I know."

"I can do it, if you want."

"We should probably do it together, just to ensure we don't miss anything."

In other words, he didn't trust her to do it correctly, thereby dooming them to being married until death did they part. She snorted and earned another side-ways look. As if that would happen.

"And we'll split the cost, of course," she said. She couldn't afford to take for granted he'd do the right thing. "Fifty-fifty."

"Yes, we'll split the cost. It should be a relatively painless process as long as we check and double-check all the boxes."

"I'm sure you're good at that."

He looked at her a long time and then reclined his seat the fraction of an inch it allowed. She did the same, wishing she'd bought a book or something in the airport. Her attempts to avoid conversation in the Uber and the airport had put a hurt on her phone's battery and she didn't want to drain it totally. Closing her eyes, she tried to occupy her mind with specials she could run for the upcoming holiday season.

She wasn't sure how much time passed before John spoke again in that terse way he seemed to reserve just for her. "You can rest your head on my shoulder."

He said it the way a man might invite a person to steal his dessert—he'll live if you do, but he'd rather you didn't. "I'm fine."

"If your head keeps jerking like that, you're going to give yourself whiplash." He leaned closer so he could whisper. "Or you'll end up sleeping on that guy's shoulder."

Chelsea shuddered. The man in the window seat, who'd put on headphones and gone to sleep immediately, reeked of old booze and a need to shower. "I'd rather not."

"It's an open invitation," John said tersely, and then he went back to reading the magazine he'd pulled out of the seat pocket.

Sometime later, Chelsea woke to find she'd taken him up on the offer. The side of her face rested against John's shoulder. And his head was resting on the top of hers. His slow, measured breathing told her he was sleeping, and she couldn't bring herself to sit up and pull her head out from under his.

He was also warm and he smelled good, and she breathed in the scent of him. Then, smiling, she closed her eyes and went back to sleep.

After a brief respite from almost constant contact with Chelsea on the plane, John found himself next to her again. And they were jammed in the backseat of Molly's little convertible, so there was no escaping the warmth and subtle floral scent coming from her body.

On the way *to* the airport Friday morning, it hadn't seemed like a big deal. Despite Callan offering his larger vehicle—and even suggesting a car service— Molly was comfortable driving in Boston and declared that taking her car would save money. John and Chelsea, whom he'd describe as his nemesis if he was asked, had ignored each other. It was as if there was a wall between them that enabled them to pretend the other didn't even exist.

Then they'd gotten married and had sex.

Apparently, that changed things because now his nerves twitched every time she moved. He heard every sigh. Every time she pushed her hair away from her face, he wanted to bury his hands in it.

It was exhausting, and all he wanted to do was get home. He'd relax, get some distance from the situation. Maybe he'd even stay home an extra day to give himself a full twenty-four hours or more without seeing Chelsea. All he needed was a reset.

His phone buzzed in his pocket and he worked to pull it free from under his seat belt. He saw *Alfred Lawrence*—his landlord—on the screen and frowned. When Alfred's wife had passed away, he'd moved in with his son and daughter-in-law in Concord. Not ready to sell the Stonefield house he'd lived in for decades, he'd chosen to rent it out, and Bruce had snapped it up for John. Alfred was friendly enough, but he wasn't the type to call and chat, which meant something might be wrong.

"It's my landlord. I need to take this." He waited until Molly had turned the music down and then hit the accept button. "Hello?"

Three minutes later he hung up and leaned forward, resting his head against the back of Molly's seat. "I thought this weekend couldn't get any worse."

"You should never think something like that," Molly said. "But what happened?"

"There was a fire at my house." He sat up straight. "They think somebody threw a cigarette butt out a window and everything's so dry right now, it basically started a fire in the leaves that had blown onto the porch."

Callan turned in his seat so he could see him. "How bad is it?"

"He said the damage is mostly to the lower front of the house—just enough so it won't be livable while they fix it. I locked everything important in the safe at work before we left. It's mostly going to be the inconvenience of not having a place to sleep."

"Can you stay with Bruce and Ann-Marie?" Callan asked.

"They don't have the room. I'd have to sleep on the couch and that's too disruptive for the girls. Maybe if it was summer and they didn't have school, but I can't ask that of Ann-Marie."

"There aren't any cheap motels nearby—or any motels, really—but we might be able to find a B&B or something," Molly suggested.

"He said it might take weeks. I can't afford that." Especially after a trip to Las Vegas, and with however much it was going to cost him to legally untangle himself from Chelsea.

"We've been slowly remodeling the upstairs bedrooms," Callan said. "If you can take Bruce's couch for now, we can probably make one of them mostly usable within a couple of days and get you out of there."

"I'm not crashing your honeymoon," John said firmly.

"Chelsea, you have a guest room," Molly said brightly. "You have a *whole house*."

The car was silent for a long moment before Chelsea answered. "Yes, I have a room. I'd rent it to you for less than other lodging would cost you."

John's instinct was to laugh and tell her he'd rather sleep on the floor of his office, but he forced himself to take a few seconds to think about it.

He definitely couldn't afford to stay in a motel or a B&B for an undetermined amount of time, especially since that would also mean restaurant meals. She opened the café early and he could stay in the office late. He'd hardly see her. And it would make coordinating their annulment process easier.

"Are you sure?" he asked her.

"I wouldn't have offered if I wasn't sure." She didn't look at him, though. And she hadn't really offered. Molly had. "We can make it work."

"Thank you. I appreciate it."

The matter appeared settled, so John sat back and watched the trees whiz by, his mind reeling. He'd gone from not caring to speak with Chelsea Grey to marrying her, sleeping with her and now, over the course of less than forty-eight hours, he'd gone to living with her.

Chapter Seven

*A message from town hall: "As many residents
(the ones who actually attend town meetings)
are aware, six months ago, we established an
email address specifically for the reporting
of problems in Stonefield. We wanted to offer
a fast, convenient way for the community to
submit complaints about minor issues, such as
potholes, parking and your neighbors sneaking
their trash bags into your collection bin. And
for those six months, we thought you all were
content and happily going about your daily
lives, but today we were informed there was a
typographical error in the address posted on
the website. We assure you this was not delib-
erate, we were not ignoring you and the email*

address has been fixed. We apologize for the inconvenience."
The Gazette *has confirmed the email address is correct now, but we urge patience while waiting for a reply because we anticipate it's going to be a very busy inbox!*
—Stonefield Gazette *Facebook Page*

They stopped at Molly and Callan's place first because John had parked his car there. On Friday Molly had picked Chelsea up at her house so they could buy a few last-minute things together and because they had limited room in their driveway. It had seemed like a good idea at the time. But now it meant she couldn't let them handle John's stuff while she raced home to make sure she hadn't left bras strewn around the place.

She hadn't, of course. Strewing bras around her house wasn't something she did, as a rule, but having a man who'd proven in the past to be highly judgmental coming into her space was making her anxious about the state she might have left it in while preparing for the Vegas trip.

After grabbing a couple of coolers and some boxes from the garage, they switched Molly's car out for Callan's bigger one and they headed for John's house. Callan rode with him, while Chelsea rode with Molly, and it was a huge relief to be alone with her friend in the quiet vehicle. Being near John used to cause a cut-and-dried tension—she didn't like him. But now it was a little more complicated. She wasn't sure that she still disliked him all that much, plus there was a buzz of sexual attraction now that hadn't faded away with the tequila buzz the way it should have.

"Are you sure you're okay with this?" Molly asked, giving her a sideways glance.

Chelsea laughed, but it was a little strange because she'd just been thinking about sex with John again. She really needed to stop doing that, period, but especially since he was going to be sleeping down the hall from her. "It's a little late now."

"No, if you're uncomfortable, we'll do something else." Molly sighed. "I got so caught up in us as a foursome and solving his problem that I forgot you guys hate each other. When you're sober, anyway."

"I think *hate* might be a strong word for it."

"I've heard *you* use it."

"Okay, that's true. But we got a chance to know each other this weekend and—"

She had to stop talking because Molly laughed so hard, Chelsea was afraid she'd drive the car right off the road. It took her friend a minute, along with some dabbing at her eyes, to get herself back under control.

"I'm sorry," Molly said, and then more laughter bubbled up. Finally, she waved her hand and tried to be serious. "You have to admit that was funny, though."

"*So* funny." Although she had walked right into that one. "Anyway, I doubt he'll ever be one of my favorite people, but I don't *hate* him. I'm not that easy to push around, so if I did hate him, he wouldn't even step inside my house, never mind sleep there."

"Maybe he could stay in Irish and Mallory's camper."

"It's November, Molly."

"Yeah, but only the first week. And it has a heater."

"I wouldn't wish a camper in the winter on anybody, even him."

Molly sighed. "I'm afraid it's going to be weird, though."

"You think?" Chelsea laughed. "It's not like he's a total stranger. I promise it's okay."

Unlike John's house. She winced when the small, blue Cape came into view, but she supposed it could have been worse. The house was definitely charred and the windows across the front had been boarded up, but it looked as if more damage had been done by the efforts to keep the whole house from burning than from the fire itself.

Once they'd parked and John had a few seconds to process the situation, Callan took charge. "We have to go in through the back door, obviously. And we don't have a lot of time because it's getting dark and all the utilities have been cut off."

"Alfred said nobody's opened the fridge, so everything should be okay," John said in a low voice. "Anything in the freezer, I'll have to let thaw and cook, though."

"We can take care of the fridge," Chelsea said,

picking up one of the coolers. "You can get anything you need from upstairs."

Going with him to his bedroom to help him pack his underwear seemed a little too intimate for Chelsea, and she'd already had more than enough intimacy with this man. She'd let Callan handle that.

It was weird, stepping into John Fletcher's house. Three days ago, if she saw him coming toward her on the sidewalk, she would have crossed the street.

The light was dimming fast, but she could see that the kitchen had been pretty immaculate before the fire department got involved. She winced when she heard the crunch of glass and smooshing sound of wet carpet as the guys carefully made their way to the stairs.

John had called the fire chief from Callan's house, just confirming Alfred's assurance he could go in if he was careful. Chelsea was skeptical, but Chief Nelson had said it was mostly broken glass in the front of the house and a lot of water damage. Structurally, it was essentially untouched.

"Oh, you're having pork chops this week!" Molly already had the freezer almost emptied while Chelsea had been looking around.

She couldn't resist poking her head into the living room. The good news was that John didn't seem to own a lot of things, so he hadn't lost much. A couch and a TV. She didn't see where any photos or art had been blown off the walls by the fire hoses. No knickknacks lying on the soaked carpet. It was beyond spartan—it was practically empty.

He'd only been there a couple of months or so, and it was a rented house, but she was still surprised he hadn't made much of an effort to make it feel like a home.

"He doesn't own any mustard," Molly said. "Is that weird? Who doesn't own mustard?"

Chelsea stopped snooping and turned her attention to the task at hand. Callan hadn't been lying—it was getting dark fast—and this would be a lot less fun done by cell phone flashlight.

It took almost an hour, but they managed to pack up everything John needed to temporarily relocate. And then they were on their way again, this time with the two vehicles full of his belongings. Which John was going to bring into her house, she thought, resting her head against the cool passenger window.

Because he lived with her now.

John had never actually seen Chelsea's house, and it surprised him because it was a lot bigger than he would have expected for a woman living alone. The cream, two-story New Englander had a deep farmer's porch and cranberry shutters. It sat on a big lot surrounded by woods, and there was a detached garage. The house was definitely one of the older ones in town, but it was in good shape.

Callan opened the back door of his car to grab a

box. "I've got a new wife I want to take home, so let's get this done."

John killed the engine and got out, grabbing the big duffel he'd packed with clothes. When he went inside, Chelsea was already going up the stairs with the laundry basket he'd tossed some shoes and toiletries into.

He had time to get a quick impression of the house—it needed updating, but it was bright and clean with no clutter and what looked like comfortable furniture—before he followed her up. She led the way to the guest room which, strangely enough, reminded him a lot of his own bedroom. Functional, comfortable, decorated in neutral shades.

There was a queen bed, and a dresser and nightstand in a pale, solid wood. An armchair that looked comfortable was in the corner, with a floor lamp behind it for reading. It was warm and welcoming, without being fussy.

"When it's not dark, this room gets good natural light," Chelsea said, and it pained him to hear the tension in her voice. "My room's on the other end of the hall. We'll have to share the upstairs bathroom, but there's also a half bath downstairs."

After listening to hear if there were footsteps on the stairs or in the hall, he stepped closer to her so he could lower his voice. But not too close because that wasn't a good idea. "This is the first time we've been alone since I got the call from Alfred. Are you *absolutely* sure this is okay?"

She snorted. "Molly asked me the same thing in the car and again, it's kind of late now."

"It's not. I can spend the night on Bruce's couch and figure out the long-term tomorrow. You and I have a history that's…not great. And I know Molly put you on the spot, but it's not too late for me to pivot."

"The way I see it, you're not an *awful* person or Molly and Callan wouldn't have you in their lives. You just seem to be a jerk where I'm concerned and if you can't help yourself and keep doing it, I'll ignore you. But I can put your rent toward my Las Vegas credit card tab."

Jerk? That seemed harsh. "I'll do my best to not be a jerk. But I want you to promise me that if at any point, you decide you don't want me here, you'll tell me. Because I'm not an *awful* person, I don't want you to be uncomfortable in your own home. This might be the easiest and most sensible option, but it's not my only one."

Something softened in her eyes and she actually smiled at him. "I promise."

Her smile knocked him sideways for a few seconds. It wasn't something she'd bestowed on him before this weekend, so he was still struggling with how it made him feel. Warm, and somehow happier than he'd been in the seconds before she smiled.

Footsteps outside the door announced Callan before he turned the corner into the bedroom. "So Molly started making room for John's stuff in your fridge, and she got distracted by the fact you don't own mustard, either, which she's taking as a sign you'll be great roommates. And now she's eating your grapes."

Chelsea laughed and started toward the door. "I'll leave you two to the heavy lifting and go help her."

When she was gone, Callan set the box he'd been carrying on the bed. "This is a nice room."

"It's a nice house," he agreed. "It's a lot bigger than I expected. I was expecting a cute cottage or... I don't know, a witch's hut or something."

Callan laughed. "From what Molly's said, she's done a lot of work to it. Not anything major, but a lot of small cosmetic touches when she could. If this had still been on the market when I moved here, I would have snapped it up in a heartbeat."

"It seems a lot for her to take care of."

"Yeah, but she probably figures she'll get married someday—on purpose, I mean—and have some kids. Or maybe she just likes a lot of space."

"Yeah." He definitely wasn't the husband she'd had in mind. "Let's get the cars unloaded so you can get your new wife home."

It took a few more trips to get everything upstairs. The cold weather meant bringing more clothes than he might have packed during the summer. Sweaters and hoodies meant bulk. He'd also taken the time to grab a few things he didn't need, but didn't want to leave in a house that would have contractors in and out, like his great-grandfather's pocket watch and accordion file that held most of his personal documents.

His move to Stonefield from Kansas City had been well planned, with everything packed in an orderly fashion. But this temporary move was chaos, and it would have given him a headache if not for the fact the mess would give him an excuse to be in the room. Even though he'd told Callan they needed to finish up so he could get his new wife home, John didn't actually want them to leave.

Once they were alone in the house, there was no way things wouldn't be awkward between him and Chelsea. What had he been thinking? He should have shown up on Bruce's door because he was his brother—he had to take him in. And Ann-Marie would have made it work, no matter how disruptive it was for Jenny and Carrie.

"I think that's it," Molly said, her hands on her hips as she looked around the room. "Unless you need help putting it all away."

"No, I'm good." He'd never find anything if he didn't put it away himself. "I really appreciate your help, though."

After Molly gave him a quick hug and Callan shook his hand, they went downstairs, leaving John alone in the bedroom. He knew he should at least make sure he could find everything he'd need for the morning, but exhaustion and an overwhelming sense of *this isn't happening* were setting in and he just stood there, listening to the faint sound of voices drifting up the stairs.

Then he heard the women laugh. The front door shut. Then car doors closing. Callan was going home with his new bride.

Leaving John alone with *his* new bride.

Chapter Eight

*Dearborn's Market and our police chief would
like to remind you that the market offers a preorder service for Thanksgiving turkeys. Stop
by or give them a call with how big or small a
bird you'll need for your family this year, and
it'll be available for you to pick up on the day
it should be transferred to your fridge for safe
thawing. November ninth is the deadline for
getting your preorder in!*

*Dearborn's is proud to be our community
market and they're doing their part to ensure
the Last-Turkey Battle of 2016 never happens
again.*

—Stonefield Gazette *Facebook Page*

Marrying him and waking up with him in her bed hadn't been enough, Chelsea thought with a pretty equal mix of bewilderment and amusement. Now John Fletcher was living with her. Temporarily, but still. Once Callan and Molly left and she was alone with John, the enormity of what she'd done hit her.

Community was important to her, though, and helping one's neighbors when they were in need was a big part of that. Plus, she wasn't going to charge him a *lot* in rent, but right now every little bit would help. She hadn't exactly budgeted for replacing Molly's wedding band and the impending legal filing.

"I guess I'm settled in," he said from behind her, startling her because she hadn't heard him come into the kitchen. It was going to take a while to get used to having somebody else in the house. "How is this going to work?"

Probably not well, she thought, but she didn't say it out loud. "In what way?"

"I don't know. Should I have my own shelf in the fridge? Are we eating meals separately or together? Do you have a routine you want me to work around?" He blew out a breath as he ran his hand through his hair. "I want you to be comfortable with this."

Comfortable living with a man she couldn't stand but had woken up married to? She wasn't sure how that was supposed to happen. But he looked so earnest that she took a deep breath and pushed down the snark.

"I get up at four." She chuckled at his grimace. "I get home midafternoon, usually. And, needless to say, I go to bed pretty early. I think the only thing we'll have to navigate is supper, and I think it would be silly to eat in shifts."

"Okay."

"It would also be silly for you to assume I'll cook for you and then do the cleaning up."

To his credit, he looked confused. "Why would I assume that?"

"It can't come as a surprise to you that a lot of men would make that assumption."

He shrugged. "Whether it's cooking or cleaning, I do my share of whatever needs doing. Plus, I actually like cooking and I'm pretty good at it."

The man cooked *and* cleaned? Other than his abrasive attitude, she couldn't imagine how he was still single—or had been before he married her, of course.

"For tonight, I was just going to make grilled cheese and tomato soup," she said. "I don't want anything too heavy because I really need to sleep easy tonight. You interested?"

"If you don't mind."

She hated the stilted tone—the overly polite way he addressed her—almost as much as she hated the terse version of him. Empathy for him softened her a little. He'd had the same rough weekend she'd had, but at least she got to be in her home now. His world was even more upside down than it had been when he woke up in her hotel room.

"Look," she said. "We've rubbed each other the wrong way in the past. And neither of us will probably ever drink tequila again. But I have some really close friends who like you a lot."

His lips twitched into an almost-smile. "And everybody tells me they can't figure out why we rub each other the wrong way because you're a really great person."

"How about we both relax and just give each other a chance. We'll go through the legal process we need to for the annulment and Alfred will fix your house and there's no reason for us to walk on eggshells the whole time."

"I'd like that," he said, giving her the entire smile this time. "What can I do to help?"

"You can make the soup while I make the grilled cheese. I like it made with milk and not water, but if you've got lactose issues or any other dietary considerations, I'm flexible."

"There's not much I won't eat."

While they worked side by side to put dinner on the table, she talked about the house. Where the washer and dryer were—unfortunately, in the basement— and where to find the vacuum cleaner—also in the basement because the old house had a serious lack of closets. She told him she was hoping to upgrade the heating system next year, but for now the house was all on one zone and she kept the thermostat on the low side. But there was a down comforter on his bed, so he'd probably be comfortable.

"I like my bedroom to be a little cool," he said. "If it's warm, you can't burrow under the covers."

If it was anybody else, her heart might have skipped a beat at being so temperature compatible, but she just smiled and cut the grilled cheese sandwiches she'd plated. She had a small table in the kitchen because she didn't see any point in buying a dining room set before she remodeled the dining room—someday— and they both opted for water to drink.

They were halfway through the meal when her filter slipped and she asked the question she'd been wondering about. "So am I your first wife?"

His jaw flexed and he gave a sharp shake of his head. "Second."

She'd asked the question lightly—almost flippantly, because it was such a ridiculous thing for a woman to have to ask her husband. And she'd expected him to chuckle in recognition of that, and also to say that yes, she was his first wife, though she didn't know why she'd made that assumption.

Now she was curious—was he divorced or widowed?—but after that tense jaw flex, she couldn't bring herself to ask. "Oh. You must have had to tell them that at the chapel, I guess, but I don't remember."

"I don't really remember much myself, but I must have told them I was divorced." His mouth twisted into a wry smile. "Or maybe I was so drunk, I forgot."

She was going to say a guy probably wouldn't get drunk enough to forget he'd had a wife before, but the man across from her had, in fact, gotten drunk enough to accidentally end up with a second wife.

"She left me for the guy who opened the new coffee shop in our neighborhood in Kansas City."

She froze with her cup halfway to her mouth. "You're joking."

"It's not really something I joke about." He set his spoon down. "And I guess that's not totally accurate. I'm the one who left, after I came home early from a business trip and found him in my bed with her."

"I'm sorry. That's awful."

"What was *really* awful was getting home late, so the house was dark. I snuck around so I wouldn't wake her, and I'd stripped down to my underwear and was about to slide into bed when the guy woke up."

Chelsea covered her mouth. "No."

He nodded. "Pam liked sleeping late, so we had blackout drapes. I was used to navigating our bedroom in the dark, so I didn't turn on any lights."

A snort of laugher escaped Chelsea, and she waved her hand. "No. I'm sorry. It's not funny *at all*, but I just imagined you actually crawling into bed with him and how shocking *that* would have been."

He chuckled. "Imagine if he didn't wake up and I just went to sleep, thinking he was Pam. That would have been a rough morning."

"Okay, so after...you decided to move to a new town and open an office next to a coffee shop?"

"Honestly, I didn't know about the coffee shop. I

knew I wanted to live here to be close to Bruce and his family, and I'd visited a few times, so I knew it was a nice town—if a little on the quaint side for me. I knew I wanted an office separate from my home, and Daphne from the real estate office handled the lease with Bruce. I signed before I visited the actual location and I never thought to ask what the neighboring businesses were."

"I wondered, actually, why you rented a whole storefront. It seems like you could easily have a home office and save a bunch of money," Chelsea said.

"I could." He dropped a bit of grilled cheese crust onto his plate and wiped his fingers on his napkin. "I moved to Kansas City because of Pam. We met in college, but that's where she was from. Our lives were full of her family and her friends."

"And she got them all in the divorce."

"Yeah. And I threw myself into work. It reached the point I rarely left my apartment and, if I did, I had nobody. I decided it would be better for me to be near my brother and his kids, and to find some balance by working outside the house."

"I know Bruce is glad you're here. It's Ann-Marie's hometown and he's been here for years, but it's not the same as having your own family nearby, I guess. But tell me something. Did—"

"I haven't told you enough?"

"Did you hate coffee *before* you found a barista in your bed?"

John laughed—not a chuckle or a low, reluctant

laugh, but the loud kind that made him throw back his head and made *her* laugh with him. He had a great laugh and she wanted to hear more of it.

"I've never liked coffee," he confessed. "But I like it even less now."

It certainly explained his attitude problem when they first met. It didn't excuse it, but at least she knew it wasn't entirely personal.

His gaze locked with hers. "How about you answer some questions now? Do you have family here?"

"No. It's just me."

He waited a few seconds and then frowned. "That's it? After I just told you the story of finding out about my wife's affair while I was in my underwear? That's not fair."

"Okay, fine." He wasn't wrong. "My dad was in the military so we moved all the time. New places, new schools. I had some aunts and uncles, but I didn't really know them because I rarely saw them. Depending on where we were stationed, it could be years in between visits. Then my parents were killed in a car accident when I was sixteen and I went to live with an uncle. His wife didn't like me, so I went to an aunt. I cost too much to take care of, so I went to live with a different aunt. Then her husband got offered a job and she told me they were moving. I didn't want to go and I was old enough to be on my own—barely—so I took off. I kept moving around, working hard, saving money and trying to decide where I wanted my forever home to be."

"And you chose Stonefield, New Hampshire?"

"Yup. I love this part of the state and the cost of living is a little lower here than in other areas nearby. Stonefield gave me a strong sense of community and they didn't have a coffee shop, so it was perfect."

"Why a coffee shop?"

She shrugged. "I worked in a few over the years— both national chains and local indies. I'm good at it— my coffee is *not* disgusting, by the way—and a good coffee shop becomes a gathering place for the town."

He nodded slowly. "I'm seeing a theme, I guess. You want the community."

"I do." After inhaling slowly to calm the emotion rising in her so she wouldn't get weepy, she managed a smile. "Nobody but me remembers my childhood. I don't have a best friend since kindergarten. I can't name a single person I graduated from high school with. I didn't go to college, so I have no roommates who remember parties and cramming for finals. My life was a blank slate when I moved here, but when I'm eighty years old, I want to be sitting in knitting club with Molly and the others and have her say 'Remember that time you had too much tequila in Las Vegas and got married?' and we'll all laugh together."

John looked at her for a long time and she couldn't tell what he was thinking. Did he not get what she meant? Or was he annoyed she'd referenced their misguided wedding?

"That must have been lonely," he said finally, in

a low voice that made her shiver. "After my divorce, when I felt like I was alone, I still had Bruce and my mom and old friends I could reach out to. I'm glad you found this place and made friends you can laugh with when you're eighty."

The kindness in his voice almost broke the hold she had on her emotions, and she needed to drag this conversation out of the deep end. "Me, too, even though I can't knit yet and Molly is convinced I'm missing the craft gene."

"My mom knits pretty obsessively, but she decided years ago that Bruce and I were too ungrateful to waste yarn on and refuses to make us anything. My nieces Jenny and Carrie have a pretty impressive collection, though."

"I've seen some of their sweaters. And the mittens. Your mom loves color." She set her spoon in her empty bowl and stood. "Speaking of your mom—"

"No," he said sharply. "I'm not telling her. The divorce was bad enough, but this…"

Another wrong turn down a conversational dark alley, she thought. She preferred to backtrack into keeping light. After taking her dishes to the sink, she looked back over her shoulder at him. "Oh, by the way, there's also no dishwasher."

Once the kitchen was cleaned—he washed and Chelsea dried and put away, since he didn't know where anything went—the awkwardness started setting in again.

"I guess I should go sort and put things away so I'm not scrambling in the morning," he said.

"Okay. I'll watch TV for a little while, but I'll probably go to bed extra early tonight. Four o'clock is bad enough when you *haven't* flown all the way to the other side of the country and back in one weekend."

"I'll be honest—I was thinking about taking an extra day off to recover. You can't stay closed for one more day? Or open late?" John knew how exhausted he was right now, and there was zero chance he could see himself waking up to a four o'clock alarm. He had no idea how she'd manage it.

"It's tempting, but I was closed for three days and I only make money if I'm actually in the café making coffee. I'll be okay. It'll take me a few nights to slowly catch up, but I'll drink a little of my profit and keep on going."

"I guess I'll see you tomorrow after work, then."

"Oh, wait." She pulled her wedding band out of her pocket and tossed it to him. "You should put that with yours. If we get around to selling them, they'll get more as a set, probably."

"Okay." He closed his fist around the ring. "Good night."

"'Night, John."

After he'd closed the bedroom door behind himself and dropped her ring onto the dresser with his, he sank onto the chair and put his head in his hands, elbows on his knees. He didn't have to get up at four o'clock, but the flights—and the events of the weekend—had knocked him for a loop and he was exhausted.

Sitting in the chair wasn't going to get stuff done, though, so he pushed himself to his feet and started with the shirts and pants on hangers that had been laid across Molly's backseat. After hanging them in the closet, he unzipped the duffel that had casual clothes, as well as socks and underwear.

He was debating on whether he should put his toiletries in the bathroom or keep them in a basket or something on the dresser when his phone buzzed.

If it wasn't for bad luck, you'd have no luck at all.

John read the text message from his brother and snorted. Bruce wasn't big on sympathy, apparently. And the next text message just furthered the point.

Heard about the fire damage. And Ann-Marie also heard you were moving your stuff into Chelsea Grey's house. Were you downing tequila nips on the plane? Is she holding you hostage? You know I have a pretty good couch.

John was tempted to call instead of texting back, but he didn't want to take the chance of ending up on speakerphone with his sister-in-law again. Also, he didn't have a good idea of how sound traveled in this house yet, and he didn't want Chelsea to overhear the conversation.

Alfred said it may take weeks and the girls have a school routine. Chelsea has a guest room.

Bruce was nothing if not practical, so he didn't expect a lot of pushback. He'd underestimated their concern for him, though, and the next message made him sit back in the chair.

Are you sure this is a good idea? We can make something work. We can put the girls together in one room and you can sleep in Jenny's bed. It's a twin but she was potty trained before we bought the mattress.

He chuckled, shaking his head. If Ann-Marie was willing to put up with trying to get the girls to share a room without fighting, they'd been talking about him and they *really* didn't think his staying with Chelsea was a good idea.

I'm good here. We're going to start the annulment process and I'm going to work a lot. And she said she could use the rent money. Thanks, though.

Five minutes later his phone chimed again and he sighed, assuming Ann-Marie had come up with another point for Bruce to pass along. But it was Callan.

How's it going?

Good here. We had a nice talk over soup and sandwiches and now I'm unpacking. Shouldn't you be paying attention to your new wife?

Who do you think told me to text you and make sure you're doing okay?

John chuckled. That sounded like Molly—always making sure the people around her were as happy as she could help them to be.

Tell her I'm good and go enjoy being newlyweds, dammit.

Callan sent back a thumbs-up emoji and John tossed the phone onto the bed, hoping that would be the last of the text messages for the night. He didn't have much else to do, but he hated typing on the phone keyboard.

He'd just finished arranging everything the way he wanted it when he heard a floorboard creaking in the hall. A few minutes later he heard the bathroom door close and then water running.

Chelsea was taking a shower.

And he was *not* going to stand in the middle of this borrowed bedroom and think about her being naked. He didn't need to imagine what she looked like without clothes. She was gorgeous enough that no amount of tequila could erase that image from his mind.

After changing into sleep pants, he plugged his

phone into the charger he'd brought and put his earbuds in. He'd listen to a podcast and maybe, if he was lucky, he'd nod off before it was over.

That was probably the only way he was going to sleep tonight.

Chapter Nine

*Notice from Stonefield Police Chief Bordeaux:
"At the suggestion of their insurance company,
the bank has updated their security, including an upgraded exterior camera. The field
of vision encompasses the gazebo in the town
square, so plan your nocturnal activities ac-
cordingly. In other relevant news, the laws regarding public indecency can be found online,
or feel free to call the station."*
—Stonefield Gazette *Facebook Page*

Chelsea wasn't feeling her best as she walked from
the small municipal parking lot to her café at dark
o'clock. It wasn't as bad as the morning she'd woken
up hungover and married, of course, but she was

groggy and having trouble shaking off the restless night.

It was weird having somebody else sleeping in her house. It was even more weird that it was John Fletcher. Oh, and he was her *husband*. It was no wonder she'd spent more of the night tossing and turning than she had sleeping.

When her alarm had finally gone off, she'd gotten ready for work as quietly as she could. Every sound she made seemed amplified in her mind, probably because she was hyperaware he was trying to sleep, so it was almost a relief to head out in the cold to open the café.

Until she saw the front. *Oh no*, she thought. *This can't be happening.*

Somebody had really gone to town celebrating Chelsea and John's surprise wedding, and they'd burned through a lot of chalk paint. *Bride* was written in huge letters on her window, and *groom* just as large on the window of Fletcher's Digital Restoration and Design. There were doodles on both, too. Wedding bells and cakes and rings. And some shapes she hoped were supposed to be bouquets, but looked slightly obscene. To top it all off, in script letters that spanned across the two windows and must have taken forever to write were the words *just married*.

It was too early for this. *Way* too early.

She'd deal with it later. Not only was it dark, but it was also too cold to stand outside scraping wedding graffiti off her window.

The routine of preparing the café soothed her. She'd worked really hard for a long time, spending as little as possible, to save up for the life she'd made for herself in Stonefield. Her coffee shop had started with the basics, but as business grew, she'd been able to add equipment until she could serve beverages that rivaled the big coffee chains.

But she made sure the Perkin' Up Café never lost the small-town vibe. She took pride in the fact she could offer lattes with foam art for the Instagram-loving crowd, but the mechanic from the garage up the street was comfortable coming in wearing his overalls, asking for a large regular coffee and getting just that.

Alma Rowell showed up five minutes after Chelsea unlocked the door, as she did every day, with a box of assorted muffins. Alma had been making muffins for the diner for years, having found a way to monetize her favorite hobby and her early hours as a farmer's wife. She'd been willing to add extra muffins to her schedule for the Perkin' Up Café. Chelsea also kept commercially bought doughnuts on hand, and that was enough for her customers. Those who wanted more than a quick snack with their coffees usually ate at home or went to the diner.

By the time her earliest commuters were served and on their way to the city for work, Chelsea was starting to shake off the events of the weekend and get into a rhythm—as long as she didn't turn around and face the window. But then Ellen Sutton and Laura Thompson walked thought the door.

"Good morning," she said. "You two are out early today."

"Chelsea!" Ellen exclaimed. "Congratulations, honey!"

She froze, not sure what to say. Of all the people in this town, Chelsea would have guessed Ellen would have already heard what happened. Her daughter, Mallory, was Molly's best friend. Two busy sons and an infant daughter had kept Mallory from going to Las Vegas, but Chelsea would bet anything Molly had kept a running text thread with her and the other Sutton sisters, Gwen and Evie, all weekend.

"It was quite a surprise," Laura said. "Last time you mentioned John to me, it wasn't flattering."

"Molly didn't tell you what happened?" Both women stared at her, eyes wide. "It was a joke."

Ellen frowned. "So you're not married."

"We are, technically." Chelsea tried not to squirm. "It was like a dare, I guess? And neither of us would back down, and there was tequila and…we're filing for annulment."

"Oh," they said at the same time.

"Yeah." She blew out a breath. "I'm not much of a drinker, so the posts online were…well, they happened. Unfortunately."

"I don't think I've ever heard of anybody playing a game of matrimony chicken before," Laura said.

"I'm confused," Ellen said. "Somebody saw John moving into your house."

"The fire," Chelsea reminded her. "He's renting my guest room until Alfred gets his repaired."

"Well, that'll take a while, knowing Alfred Lawrence. There was nowhere else John could stay?"

"Not without inconveniencing somebody."

Laura nodded. "Bruce doesn't really have the room. And the girls have school. It's so hard to mess with routines when they're that age."

"It's all just a mistake and a coincidence at the same time, I guess."

"But on the plus side," Laura said. "Your story is a lot more interesting than mine, so there won't be anybody left talking about me and Riley."

Chelsea scoffed. "I think everybody already moved on from that."

Laura had become the hot topic in Stonefield when she started dating a younger man who'd just been hired by her son and nephew to work for their tree service. It had been a little bit of a scandal, but a drunken wedding in Las Vegas between two people who were known to dislike each other was definitely going to knock Laura and Riley off the front page.

"You know," Ellen said thoughtfully. "Alcohol lowers the inhibitions and encourages people to say or do things they're afraid to say sober."

"Oh!" Laura's eyes lit up. "That's true, so maybe you and John secretly wanted to hook up and this dare thing gave you the excuse."

"No." Sure, John was very attractive. There was no denying that. But there had been friction between them from the start—and not the good kind. "Trust me. He and I were not secretly lusting after each other."

"Who knows this wasn't supposed to end at the altar?" Ellen asked. "I mean everybody saw or heard about your posts—especially the hashtags—but this is the first I've heard you'll be getting an annulment."

Chelsea sighed. "Honestly, I expected everybody to know by the time we landed in Boston. Molly knew, so I thought that was a safe assumption."

"To be fair, she was busy getting married herself," Laura pointed out.

"True. So, coffee?" Chelsea asked in a too-chipper voice, desperate to get out of the conversation.

She'd been relying on Stonefield's usually ruthlessly efficient whisper network to spread the word about the joke going too far. And then there were the windows she didn't have time to deal with. Customers would keep coming in and congratulating her, and she would have to offer her vague, awkward explanation every time, so it was going to be a long day.

Once Ellen and Laura had their drinks and were seated at a table, Chelsea picked up her cell phone. John was still listed in her contacts as *hubby*, but she'd deal with that later. She typed out a message.

There's been some kind of disruption in the town's gossip network. Even Ellen Sutton and Laura Thompson hadn't heard we didn't really mean to get married. Maybe we should submit a news item to the Gazette's Facebook Page.

She set her phone down when another customer came in—another customer who congratulated her and then looked slightly let down upon learning it was all a misunderstanding of sorts. And then two more customers after that.

When her phone chimed, she picked it up and read John's reply.

No.

She frowned at the screen. That was it? Just…*no*? There was that John Fletcher she'd never been able to stand.

Even though she hadn't really been serious about the Gazette thing, she didn't like his high-handedness. The state of Nevada might think she was his wife, but he was *not* the boss of her. Nobody was. She could do what she wanted, even sending a confusing and personally embarrassing news item to the local newspaper. But if he wanted to play monosyllabic word tag, she'd play.

Why?

She wasn't sure he'd respond at all, but his message came through quickly and it was more than one word.

Why don't I want a particularly humiliating moment in my personal life advertised in the town's newspaper AGAIN? Do I really need to answer that?

She was still trying to compose a response that didn't include expletives and that wouldn't escalate the snark to a new level—they were temporarily living together, after all—when another text came through.

Let me rephrase, please. I would prefer not to post anything publicly. The wedding announcement was bad enough, but the drunken mistake stuff would be there for anybody to read, forever. Maybe we can see if the news spreads organically now that Ellen and Laura know. Or you could even enlist their help, if you know what I mean.

The tension eased out of her, and she was thankful he'd walked back the attitude. Having him under her roof was awkward enough without open hostility between them again.

An excellent plan, she typed back. I'm on it.

It was strange, being a guest in the home of somebody who didn't like you very much and was also your wife.

Wife.

John dried the few dishes he'd made having breakfast and put them away where he'd found them, a mindless task that allowed his mind to keep wandering back to the situation he'd found himself in. It was still hard to believe, but he not only—temporarily—had a wife, but he also—temporarily—lived with her.

He'd just gotten out of the shower when he got the text message from her about the town not getting the message about their marriage not actually being a love match for the ages. The bit about sending a notice to the *Stonefield Gazette* had thrown him and he'd sent a terse response before realizing she'd probably been joking.

Hopefully, enlisting Ellen and Laura would help. He didn't really want him and Chelsea to have to explain the situation to each person they ran into individually. Those two women, plus Molly and her circle, should take care of the problem, which helped improve his mood.

By the time he'd found a place to park—well away from the café because he didn't care to be towed again—he felt ready to get some work done.

Then he saw his window.

Groom? Just married?

John stared at the unsolicited—and very unwelcome—additions to his window. Why hadn't Chelsea given him a heads-up when she was texting him earlier? Maybe she'd been about to when he'd sent the terse response and she'd decided not to. That would be petty, but he wouldn't put it past her. Just because she'd agreed to rent him a room and they'd shared some soup didn't mean they were suddenly friends now.

Maybe he could ignore it until the end of the day. Since it was unlikely the culprit had decorated the windows in the middle of the night, half the town had probably seen it yesterday. And the other half had no doubt heard about it. Rushing to clean it off wouldn't save him any embarrassment at this point.

It could wait until he'd finalized and sent the graphics package his client was waiting for. It wasn't due until the end of the week, but he hadn't foreseen a trip to Las Vegas and a small house fire when he agreed to the deadline. There was still plenty of time, but he didn't like a ticking clock pressuring him. After unlocking the door and turning on the lights, he fired up his computer.

But when he sat in his chair and looked over the top of the monitor, that window was directly in his line of vision.

M-O-O-R-G.

It was a distraction, to say the least. Every time he happened to glance up, he saw that backward *groom* and thought about the fact he was legally a married man. That made him think about Chelsea. And from there it was a downhill slide into staring off into space, trying like hell to unearth memories of their wedding night.

He remembered more of it than he'd let on to others. Not wanting to make Chelsea even more uncomfortable was part of why he kept it to himself. And it was nobody else's business, of course.

Mostly, though, it was because the fractured memories—his mouth on her breast, the feel of her hands on his body and the sound of his name on her lips—were like treasures he was hoarding.

Nope.

John pushed back his chair and stood. There was no way he was going to get any work done sitting around thinking about the way Chelsea had giggled when he kissed the inside of her thigh.

He'd clean the window first. Once he'd wiped the glass clean of the misguided messaging, he'd be able to focus. Hopefully.

Unfortunately, he didn't have anything that would get the job done without smearing the window chalk into a bigger mess. He kept basic cleaning supplies in the tiny bathroom, but he'd run out of glass cleaner and buying more was on his to-do list. Screen-cleaning wipes definitely wouldn't cut it.

He knew Chelsea had stuff made for the purpose, though. She liked to write specials and funny coffee puns on her window. He'd brushed against the glass while the chalk paint was still wet once, trying to give space to a woman wrangling three kids and a dog, and pastel pink paint had smeared down his sleeve.

Chelsea had been furious and actually accused him of ruining her window art as payback for her having his car towed. He told her that was ridiculous, which she took as him calling *her* ridiculous. The next day somebody "accidentally" spilled hot chocolate on the sidewalk in front of his door and it was sticky for days. Yeah, she could be petty if she wanted.

Remembering that day—along with a lack of sleep—made him yank the café's door open with a little more force than he'd intended.

Chelsea turned as the bell made a choked clanging sound, her brow furrowing. "I'd say good morning, but it's clearly not."

"Sorry," he muttered, nodding his head toward the bell. "But I feel like you could have warned me about the windows."

"I didn't want to ruin the surprise."

"I think I've had enough surprises this week." He was about to say more when he realized his entrance had drawn the attention of several customers sitting in the café and they were all staring at them.

He moved to the counter, close enough to talk to Chelsea in a low voice so nobody else in the café would hear him. He hoped. Between the trip to Las Vegas and the fire, he was over his fifteen minutes of fame in this town.

"I came to borrow whatever it is you use to clean that stuff off the windows."

"I have stuff, and I was planning to clean it off after I close, even though I change my window on Wednesdays."

"I don't know if I can look at it that long."

"Until midafternoon? I think you'll live."

"You can do yours whenever, but if you lend me the stuff, I'll clean mine off now."

She shrugged. "Suit yourself, but it's messy and it takes longer than you think."

John sighed, thinking about it. As much as he didn't want to look at the wedding decorations for the rest of the day, he also didn't want to track the stuff all over his office. He'd never worked with window chalk, and he'd probably end up making a pretty big mess. He'd also planned to work.

"Okay, I'll wait." He nodded, and then changed the subject. "Why Wednesdays?"

"What?"

"Why do you change your window on Wednesdays?"

"Because it's my slow day, so it gives me something to do." Her mouth curved into a smile and he tried to ignore the way it made his heart beat a little faster. "And people look to see what it says and some of them come in. It's a nice midweek pick-me-up."

"Smart." He frowned. "My window's boring."

"Not right now," she said, and he chuckled. The windows weren't funny, but she was, and he appreciated that in a person. "I've had a suggestion for your window for a while, but I didn't think you'd welcome my input."

"I probably wouldn't have," he admitted. "But it'll give us something to talk about over supper, I guess."

"Better than awkward silence," she said, and they shared a smile.

"Did you talk to Ellen and Laura?" he asked.

"I did. Word should spread pretty quickly now that they know. I don't know why Molly didn't say anything to the Sutton sisters. It's weird." She shrugged. "I think she was amused by it, which is better than being mad about it, and didn't want the fun to end."

"Definitely a possibility." He nodded. "I guess I'll go back to work, then. It's not easy to concentrate with *groom* written on my window in massive letters, though. I might have to turn my desk around."

She laughed. "Want a drink for the road? I do offer things besides coffee, you know."

He looked at the chalk menu board. "I drink tea sometimes. In the winter, usually, when I want a hot drink, but don't want all the hot cocoa sugar."

"I've got just the thing. Give me a few minutes and I'll deliver it to you." He started to pull out his wallet, but she shook her head. "This one's on the house. I'm going to make you a fan of this café."

"Challenge accepted," he said, and he was smiling when he walked out the door.

A few minutes later his door opened and Chelsea walked in, carrying a glass mug filled with a creamy-looking beverage topped with foam.

"That looks like a latte," he pointed out.

"It's a London Fog latte," she said, setting the glass down on his desk. "Earl Grey. Vanilla. Trust me. You'll love it."

She was gone before he could take a sip, and he was glad of that once he tasted the beverage. If she'd seen his expression, there would have been no living with the gloating.

Chapter Ten

A lost dog found his way to the fire station this morning. If you've lost a terrier mix, he'll be waiting for you in the care of Chief Nelson. Please hurry because, according to the chief, he's a cute little guy and Mrs. Nelson is allergic to dogs. He'd hate to have to choose.
          —Stonefield Gazette *Facebook Page*

"Okay, tell me about your idea for my window," John said once they were seated at the kitchen table with the hamburger steaks and gravy he'd made.

Chelsea took a bite first and yes, the man could definitely cook. "I assume most of your graphic design work is internet-based, and local business would be more photo restoration?"

He nodded. "For the most part, yes."

"Okay. I get the impression from being in your office today that you like a clean aesthetic, but if it was *my* business, I'd showcase what I do more. You have some examples inside, but I think you should have some in the window. A before photograph and then the restored version. People will stop and look at them, and a lot of them have old photos tucked away. Seeing what you can do with them would be a big draw."

She watched him think about what she said for a moment, and then he nodded slowly. "You're right."

"And I wouldn't make them all really old photos or complicated. Like, maybe just showing a photo that got folded and you can fix it would be cool. Let people know it doesn't have to be a big project."

"I didn't think of that—that people might think their photo isn't a big or special enough project to bring to me. Thanks."

"No problem. And thank you for this dinner. It's delicious." The smile he gave her made her quiver inside, and she turned her eyes back to her gravy-smothered potatoes.

She'd been more optimistic about the roommate situation now that they were more than twenty-four hours in, but the warmth in that smile gave her pause. Things between them weren't as awkward as she'd feared they would be, but that wasn't necessarily a good thing. Awkwardness would drive them to avoid each other as much as possible, and if they were avoiding each other, he wouldn't be able to smile at her like that and she wouldn't think about things she was better off not thinking about.

She absolutely could not let on that her attraction to him didn't seem to have stemmed wholly from the tequila.

As soon as the kitchen was clean, she told him she was behind on her book club reading and he was welcome to the television before practically fleeing to her bedroom.

It was just a smile, she told herself so many times before turning off her light, she lost count. He was a friendly guy, despite her initial impression of him, and friendly guys smiled. It was no big deal.

And yet, an image of him smiling was the first thing that popped into her head when her alarm went off at four o'clock. She staggered through getting ready for work and was almost awake by the time Alma dropped off the muffins and her first customer walked through the door.

The man didn't even have to be in bed with her to blow her sleep schedule all to hell.

When she looked out the window and saw Molly crossing the street, heading for her door, she sighed. Usually, visits from her friend were one of her favorite things about owning the café—people could stop in and see her any time they wanted. But she was low on energy today and sometimes Molly was a lot.

Still, her smile was genuine when Molly walked

in, and she gave her a little wave. "Good morning, Mrs. Avery."

Molly's face brightened, and she was obviously still delighted by her newlywed status. "We've decided we're going to be Mr. and Mrs. Avery-Cyrs. It'll be a lot of paperwork, but it makes us both happy."

"I love that! He's changing his, too?"

"Yeah, so we'll match. Isn't that the sweetest? And our names sound good together, too." She paused a moment before briefly covering her mouth to stifle a giggle. "Fletcher-Grey sounds like a special, limited-edition tweed color."

Chelsea groaned. "We are *not* changing our names. But speaking of Mr. and Mrs., any idea who decorated our windows?"

She laughed. "No, but I wish I did."

"I know you talked to Mallory, at least, and probably Gwen and Evie, too, while we were in Vegas. Why didn't you tell them we didn't mean to get married? Then Ellen would have found out and John and I probably wouldn't have shown up to *just married* written across our windows."

"I did tell Mal, actually. But it was late and she's got two boys to run to activities, plus a baby. Her memory's not running on all cylinders at the moment. She probably meant to tell them." Molly looked past Chelsea's shoulder.

"It took me forever to get all that window chalk off, by the way. Anyway, what are you drinking today?"

"Surprise me. Have you finished the Books & Brews book yet?"

"Not yet." It seemed like a caramel macchiato day for Molly. "Did you?"

"No, but it's not until tomorrow night. Still plenty of time. Did I tell you my mom didn't want to watch the wedding video the minute I was home? She said we're going to watch it a week from today because that's when she has time. Like I don't have access to her calendar? I think she's punishing me for getting married in Las Vegas."

It was actually because they were going to watch it at a surprise party Molly's mom had organized at the Sutton house, but Chelsea had to admit Amanda hadn't come up with a good cover story. She probably should have watched it with Molly and then watched it again with the rest of the women. Maybe she *was* punishing her, a little bit.

She'd just handed Molly her drink when more customers came in. Molly took her notebook and went to her favorite table. Chelsea knew she'd work on some notes and planning while she sipped her coffee, and then she'd wander over to the library to see her husband if she didn't have anything pressing to do.

Once she'd taken care of everybody's orders, Chelsea asked Molly to keep an eye on things for a minute so she could run to the restroom. She'd been drinking a lot of water, trying to flush the rich foods and alcohol of Vegas out of her system, and maybe she'd had a little too much.

When she returned, she found Molly behind the counter, talking to Margaret from the police station. Molly looked flustered and her cheeks were pink, but Margaret was just chatting.

"Thanks, Molly," Chelsea said, taking her usual place as Molly went back to the customer side of the counter. Her laptop was open, which was odd, but maybe Molly had been looking something up when Margaret entered. Random questions often popped into her friend's head and she'd drop everything to find the answer *right that minute*.

"I need to see about getting a gift card for Chief Bordeaux," Margaret said. "He lost a bet."

Chelsea waved goodbye to Molly, who was heading out the door, before giving Margaret a confused look. "My coffee is the punishment for losing a bet?"

The other woman laughed. "No. I'm sorry that came out wrong. Chief Bordeaux lost a bet and the winner wants a Perkin' Up Café gift card as payment."

"I like the sound of that much better. What was the bet?"

"I'm not at liberty to say."

Chelsea waited for her to laugh again, but apparently, she was serious. "Okay, then. Let's get you that gift card."

The rest of the day was busier than an average Tuesday, which made Chelsea happy. Not only because a lot of business meant more money, but also because it made the time fly by. She never napped if she could help it—one of the downsides of having to go to bed early—but today she might break that self-imposed rule.

When she pulled into her driveway, a pile of boxes on her porch caught her eye and she frowned. They were probably the Christmas cups she'd ordered for the café, but they should have been delivered there and not to her home address. As she climbed the steps, she debated on whether to put them in her car or wait and let John help her.

There were definite upsides to having a man around the house.

But then she realized there were multiple boxes of various sizes, and none were from her distributor. The first two she picked up were addressed to her, but then she saw the mailing label on the biggest box.

Mr. & Mrs. John Fletcher.

After a very frustrating workday thanks to a client who couldn't decide on a color palette, John walked through Chelsea's front door and dropped his keys next to hers on the table in the hall. Whatever she was cooking smelled amazing and he inhaled deeply as he toed off his shoes and nudged them onto the mat next to the sneakers Chelsea favored for work.

He found her in the kitchen. She was standing at the island, looking at various boxes piled in front of her. It looked as if she'd knocked over a Bed, Bath & Beyond and this was her loot.

"Two questions," he said when she looked up from

a good-sized box. "One—and most importantly—what smells so good? And second, what's all this?"

"It's just chicken tenders. My favorite recipe, and super easy to make."

"I haven't even tried them, but I can tell by the smell I'm going to want that recipe." He'd been hungry when he left the office, but now he was downright ravenous. "So did you rob a housewares department after you closed the café?"

"There were some boxes, which I thought were the Christmas cups I ordered. Turns out they're wedding presents."

"Oh." It hadn't even occurred to him people would buy them gifts. Based on the timing, people woke up Saturday morning, saw her social media posts and placed orders online by lunch. "You have generous friends."

"Actually, *we* do. One of the perks of living in such a small town is that postal workers and delivery drivers always know where to find you. There are also a couple of things sent in care of your brother, so Ann-Marie must have dropped them off." She held up a box with a picture of a coffee grinder on it. "Do you know a Phil and Brenda?"

He nodded. "He's my cousin I haven't seen in two years. Thanks for tagging my business in your Facebook post, by the way, to ensure everybody saw it."

"You're welcome." She snorted. "I figured it had to be somebody on your side because buying me a coffee grinder is kind of funny."

"Buying *me* a coffee grinder isn't any less funny, really." He leaned in, looking the boxes over. "Is that a heated towel rack?"

"Yes, and we're sending it back."

"Technically, we *did* get married," he said, grinning.

"Is there a cutoff date for how long the marriage has to go on before you get to keep the gifts?"

He frowned, pretending to think about it. "If annulment means the marriage never existed, do the presents just become regular gifts and not wedding gifts?"

She laughed. "I wish. People were very generous before word got out."

"Who gave us that toaster oven?" Even though he knew they were just joking around, it struck him how absolutely typical their conversation sounded. Somebody eavesdropping might even mistake them for a real married couple.

"The Dearborns. They're so sweet."

He watched her run her hand over the box, and then she gave him a speculative look before looking at the box again. "Chelsea Grey, are you considering staying married to me so you can keep that toaster oven?"

"It's a really nice toaster oven, John." She turned the box so he could see it. "Look at all the functions it has."

"What else did we get?"

She laughed and slapped at the hand he reached toward the pile. "A bunch of stuff I have to return now, which means contacting everybody to thank them, but letting them know we'll be sending gifts back."

"That *we* have to return," he corrected, and then the oven timer dinged. "We can make a list after we eat and then divide it up based on who we each know the best."

"At least you'll have a reason to reach out to your cousin."

He gave her a look. "Phil is the reason Bruce's nose is slightly crooked. And he also *knows* I don't like coffee."

How did she have such a cute scowl? "How about we give the coffee grinder to Bruce and Ann-Marie, and we just let Phil and Brenda think you're happily married?"

"Tempting." He'd return it, of course, but her revenge plan did amuse him and he smiled as he set the table.

The chicken was as good as it smelled, and she'd made a salad to go with it. Unfortunately, the gifts piled on the island were in his line of sight—visible reminders he wasn't just sharing a meal with a woman who was, much to his surprise, becoming a friend.

He was eating supper with his wife.

She told some amusing stories from the early days of the Perkin' Up Café while they ate and cleaned up. He knew she was sharing them to fill the silence without having to talk about their situation, and he appreciated that. He also chuckled several times while she talked about having to explain lattes and macchiatos and espresso so many times she'd put a *Coffee 101* graphic on her Facebook Page.

Once they were done putting the dishes away, she found a notebook and pen. They made a list of the gifts and who had sent them and their initials next to who was responsible for dealing with each. There was a lot of overlap, though, so they divided those evenly.

"Sending this toaster oven back is going to hurt," she said when they were done. "Once the legal costs are behind me, I'm going to start saving for one."

And just like that, the elephant was back in the room. The process for annulment had turned out to be more complicated than they thought, so with his agreement, she'd hired a legal outfit in Nevada that specialized in cases like theirs. It would cost a little more, but they didn't want to screw it up and end up *actually* married.

John cleared his throat. "Yeah. I'm going to go downstairs and grab my laundry, and then take it upstairs and put it away."

She nodded. "Laundry day is definitely a workout."

"It's a big house. If I wore one of those step counters, it would probably be pretty proud of me."

"It *is* big and sometimes, like when the heating bills come in, I wonder what I was thinking." She looked around the kitchen and then she smiled. "Then

I remember that no matter what life brings, I won't outgrow this home."

Because she's going to live in this spot for the rest of her life. He envied her the stability of that dream, but he still had a hard time wrapping around wanting to spend decades in Stonefield. Sometimes a guy just wanted egg rolls delivered at midnight.

Chapter Eleven

*With Thanksgiving around the corner, we
thought it would be fun to do a quick poll: Do
you like your cranberry sauce with whole ber-
ries or do you like it jellied? The* Gazette *staff
is split, fifty-fifty, so let us know in the comments which you prefer!*
—Stonefield Gazette *Facebook Page*

The following evening Chelsea pushed back her empty
plate and stifled a yawn. "Delicious pork chops, John.
Thank you."

"You look beat."

If she confessed she was having trouble sleeping, he might ask her why and she didn't really want
to tell him it was because she was thinking about

their night in Vegas instead of sleeping. "It was slow today, which is sometimes as tiring as being busy. It makes the day drag on, which is not ideal when you get up at four."

"Have you considered not being open seven days a week?"

"I've considered it several times, but it doesn't make sense. There really isn't a good day to be closed. And it's not like I have anything better to do, so I may as well make money."

"What about Wednesdays? You said that's your slow day."

"What good is a Wednesday off, though? Everybody else will be at work. But for several months I've been considering not opening until seven on weekends. I'm probably losing money on those four hours per week because most of the early-morning commuters are Monday through Friday."

"That makes sense, though I still think working seven days a week must be hard. I mean, I get it. I'm self-employed, too. But I try to have at least one entire day off each week."

"Someday I'd like to find somebody to work parttime, like somebody who only wants to work weekends. In the meantime, if there's something I really want to do—like going to Las Vegas for Molly's wedding—I just close and take the hit." She shrugged. "Since we're talking about business, I get the graphic design part, but how did you get into restoring old photographs?"

"Not always old. Sometimes damaged. I've even

taken junk out of backgrounds. One time a woman brought me her cell phone and she'd captured the most gorgeous shot of her granddaughter and she wanted to print and frame it for her daughter, but it was taken at a park and there was litter and stuff ruining it."

"But what got you interested in the first place?"

"When I was in middle school, I was teaching myself how to do graphic design. I ended up with a degree in it, of course, but the foundation was self-taught. Anyway, my mom lost her parents when she was young, and then there was a fire in the apartment she lived in shortly before she met my dad. All she had left of them was a family photo taken at a barbecue when my mom was ten."

She barely managed to refrain from reaching across the table to squeeze his hand "That's so sad."

"I never knew them, of course, but it made Mom sad. And that photo was creased and had some water spots. It took me a long time to restore it, since I was learning skills as I went, but I finally got a copy worth printing. I'll never forget the look on her face when I gave it to her. And that's when I realized how much photographs really matter."

"We don't think memories fade," she said. "We think we'll always remember, but faces and events get blurry over time."

"So true."

She glanced at the clock on the stove. "Crap. I need to hurry because I've got Books & Brews tonight, and I don't want to miss this one because it was one of Molly's picks. I want to yell at her about the love interest dying at the end in person."

"I can clean up."

"Nope. You cooked. I'm going to clean up," she said, standing and taking her plate to the counter. "It's only fair."

"I'll help. I don't want your time giving Molly a hard time to be cut short." He chuckled. "Callan said she picks books she knows will be controversial in some way because it makes the conversations more fun."

"That's our Molly." She started filling the sink with hot, soapy water. "He hasn't talked you into joining yet?"

John shook his head as he scraped his plate into the trash. "He tried, but I read what I'm in the mood to read. Reading a book I don't care about so I can go sit and argue about it with a bunch of other people doesn't sound like a good time to me."

"We don't always argue. Sometimes we agree."

"And that sounds boring."

She laughed because he wasn't wrong. "I don't know if you can fully assimilate into a small town if you're not willing to argue with your neighbors about what the author meant by making the protag-onist's car blue."

"I'm only here for a year, so I'll probably survive."

Chelsea didn't stop washing the plate, but on

the inside she felt as if she'd frozen. "What do you mean?"

"The leases on the house and the office space— they're for one year."

"And then you'll extend them if you haven't found a better location?"

He shrugged. "I don't think so. I'm more of a city guy. I wanted to spend some time in—or very close to—Stonefield to reconnect with Bruce and my nieces, but I don't see myself here long-term."

"Oh." He'd never mentioned that. And she hadn't heard it through the grapevine, either. It seemed odd that Callan hadn't mentioned it, considering they were best man-level friends.

"I'm not really interested in Boston," he continued. "But I could see myself living in Concord or Portsmouth."

He was leaving.

Chelsea's face flushed and she kept her back to John so he wouldn't notice and ask her what was wrong. Or, even worse, guess what it was.

Even though they absolutely had to go through with the annulment, she'd been toying with the possibility the end of their marriage didn't have to mean the end of their friendship. Once they'd been forced together by tequila and a house fire, she'd discovered she actually liked him. He was a surprisingly nice guy, very sexy and he cooked and cleaned. Maybe they could try *actually* dating.

Thank goodness she hadn't said any of that out loud. To anybody.

"Since you like cities so much," she said, "do you have plans for after work tomorrow?"

"Not really. Have something fun in mind?"

She laughed. "Fun? Not so much. But necessary. I'm going to Concord to do my once-a-month shopping. I try to give most of my business to Dearborn's—especially after the toaster oven—but when it comes to stuff like laundry detergent and staples I buy in bulk, I can't afford *not* to make the trip."

"I can finish a little early at the office and go with you. I need a few things, too, and it's only fair."

"Then it's a—" She broke off as she dried her hands. She'd almost said *date*. "Plan."

The doorbell rang, startling her. She wasn't expecting any deliveries, and if it was one of her friends, they would have sent a text message before stopping by.

"Damn, I forgot to tell you Callan said he'd stop by. He was supposed to come to my office with that form, but he got held up, so he said he'd bring it over."

She nodded, and John went to answer the door. *That* form had to do with Chelsea—whom they'd decided would be the official filer—letting John know her intent to have their marriage annulled. Callan just had to sign an affidavit of service saying he gave John the document, and where and when. The whole thing made Chelsea's head hurt, and she could only hope the firm they'd hired wasn't leading them astray. Of course the first thing they'd learned was how simple the process would have been if they'd skipped the breakfast buffet and taken care of it first thing the next morning.

"Hey, Molly," she said when her friend walked into the kitchen. "John didn't tell me you were coming, too."

"Probably because he didn't know until he opened the door." She grinned. "I like to be a surprise."

"The best kind of surprise." She glanced at the clock on the microwave. "But what about Books & Brews?"

"We still have time. Let's sneak upstairs to your room while they take care of that paperwork."

Chelsea was confused. "Upstairs? Why?"

"So we can talk privately." Molly dropped her voice to a dramatic whisper. "You know, about marriage stuff."

"Okay." It seemed a little odd, but if her favorite newlyweds were already going through a rough patch, she wanted to be a safe place for Molly.

She led the way, but they had to pass by the living room to get to the stairs. Both men looked up from the form Callan was filling out at the coffee table.

"I need Molly's opinion on a dress I bought," Chelsea said, trying to sound natural. It seemed John wasn't the only one good at coming up with on-the-spot lies.

"I guess we're going to be here a while," Callan said, but the look he gave Molly was full of amused affection. They didn't look at each other like they were having marital woes.

Once they were in Chelsea's room, Molly closed the door and then looked around as if she'd never seen it before. She had, though, last year. Molly had read or watched something and gone on a decluttering binge that had extended to her friends. They'd spent two whole evenings in this room while Molly made her touch everything in her closet and dresser, and discard or donate anything that didn't bring her joy.

Chelsea didn't really care about clothes outside of functionality and comfort—snuggly pajamas being the exception, of course—and she'd been in jeopardy of not having enough clothes left to get through a week before she begged off.

"What's going on?" Chelsea finally asked when Molly wandered toward the bedside table. "What *marriage stuff* are you going through?"

"Me? Nothing. We're super happy and not going through any stuff. I meant *your* marriage."

She blew out a breath. "Funny, Molly. My marriage is a temporary mistake we're in the process of fixing, which you know, since that's literally why you're here right now."

"Is he really sleeping in the guest room?"

Surprise made her bark out a laugh. So that was why Molly had been looking around. She was looking for evidence of John in her bedroom. "Of course he's sleeping in the guest room. I didn't rent him the other half of my bed."

"That's disappointing."

"You know John and I don't get along." Maybe they were now, but sharing that wouldn't help Chelsea's case here. "He had a fire and I have a guest room. It was the neighborly thing to do and that's all there is to it. Well, besides the rent."

Molly didn't look convinced. "You're living with somebody you supposedly don't like, but you've been in a good mood. Callan says John's been in a good mood, and he hasn't been staying late at the office like we thought he would just to avoid you—because you go to bed so early—so we just assumed you were…you know. And the vibe in this house is *not* tense."

"Maybe we've been forced to get to know each other and we both realized we got off on the wrong foot. There's a lot of space between hating each other and sleeping together."

"Okay, so you're getting to know each other. Maybe once your marriage is annulled, you can start dating."

"You don't quit, do you?" Chelsea turned to her dresser, using the task of taking her earrings out and putting them in a glass dish to hide her face. She didn't want Molly to guess she'd been thinking about that very thing before she and Callan arrived.

And before she found out John didn't want to still be living in Stonefield by this time next year.

"I'm not going to date John Fletcher," she said firmly. "It's never going to happen."

* * *

"Must be quite the discussion about the dress," John said, looking up at the ceiling as if he could see through the floor and see what was taking them so long. "They've been up there awhile."

Callan actually laughed out loud at him. "You believed that?"

"There's no dress?"

"Thanks to Molly sharing every detail of the Vegas trip planning with me—and I do mean every single detail—I happen to know Chelsea owns two dresses. One is the red one that you may or may not remember."

Oh, he remembered the red dress. There wasn't enough booze in Vegas to erase the memory of how she looked that night. He wished he had a clearer memory of stripping it off her, though.

"And she has a black one for funerals and any other occasions the red one wouldn't be appropriate." Callan held up his hand when John opened his mouth. "I know, but trust me—Molly was very invested in Chelsea's dress situation, so I heard all about it. When Molly showed her the pink dress she wanted her to wear, Chelsea was pretty adamant she already owned two dresses, and she didn't need three."

"So why the subterfuge?"

"Knowing my wife, she wanted to get into Chelsea's room to look for evidence you're sleeping in there with her."

John scrubbed his hand over his face. "I'm not."

"Yet." When John gave him a look, Callan chuckled.

Standing, John stretched and then looked toward the ceiling again. Molly amusing herself was one thing, but it was Chelsea who'd coughed up the dress excuse. What had *she* thought they were going to talk about?

"Any idea how long this will take?" Callan asked, and John turned to see him holding the affidavit of service.

"It shouldn't be more than a couple of weeks, according to the lawyer. It's pretty straightforward. We were both too drunk to give legal consent, and neither of us is going to contest the annulment. We definitely haven't acquired any communal property in the last few days, since we didn't keep the toaster oven."

"Molly told me Chelsea wanted to keep that toaster oven, and I guess she asked Ellen to let her know if they get one in at the thrift store."

"I wrote down the model information so I can maybe catch one on sale," John admitted.

"So then what?"

John frowned, not understanding the question. "Then I'll make pizza rolls, or maybe some chicken nuggets."

Callan snorted. "I mean after the legal stuff is done with."

"That's it. When the annulment is official, it's as if it never happened. There's no more to do."

"So you'll just go back to your house and you'll work next door to each other like Vegas never happened?"

It finally dawned on him what Callan was hinting at and he shook his head. "Yes. Do you want to come see a shirt I bought so you can see if I'm really sleeping in the guest room?"

Callan had the grace to look slightly embarrassed. "Sorry. Molly's got me all wrapped up in her idea you two are a perfect couple."

It wasn't the worst idea she'd ever had, but Callan and Molly were ignoring two very important pieces of the puzzle. One, they weren't a couple. Sure, he felt a sizzle of not just attraction, but *awareness* every time she walked into the room. And obviously, when alcohol shut down their inhibitions, they were attracted to each other. He spent a lot of time thinking about that. But they weren't a real couple.

And two, he didn't intend to stay in Stonefield long-term, and Chelsea had deliberately chosen the town to set down deep roots in. He'd already figured out there was no future in that for the two of them, and he was glad he'd caught it now.

He was saved from having to continue the awkward conversation by the women returning downstairs. He noticed Chelsea didn't make eye contact, which made him wonder what the hell they'd been talking about up there. If Molly hadn't been any more subtle interrogating her than Callan was with him, it was no wonder things were awkward.

"What did you think of the dress?" he asked Molly, unable to resist the opportunity to poke at Chelsea.

It visibly took her a few seconds to remember what he was talking about, and then she gave a mournful shake of her head. "I told her she should return it because it's brown. Who wants to wear a brown dress?"

Chelsea snorted, giving her friend a sideways look. "Not everybody shares your love of color, but yes, I'm returning the brown dress. I don't know what I was thinking. I need to finish that kitchen before I head to the taproom. Though I don't suppose I can be considered late to book club if you're both still here. If you stay, I can skip it and go to bed early."

"You know, you should have opened a decaf shop," Molly said. "Then you wouldn't have to open until two o'clock in the afternoon."

"But I'd have to stay open until late, plus I'd be broke because I know this town's caffeine habits and Stonefield would *not* support a decaf shop."

John watched Molly think about it—as if she was actually trying to calculate the odds of a shop dedicated to decaffeinated coffee surviving in Stonefield—and then Callan laughed and put his arm around her shoulders. "We need to get to the taproom before you decide to open a decaf shop to compete with your friend's coffee shop and we're late to our own book club."

"But we'd be open different hours," she argued as her husband steered her toward the door.

Goodbyes were said, and John was chuckling as they pulled out of the driveway. "Poor Callan's worried he'll have to drink decaf for the rest of his life."

"By the time they get to Sutton's Place, she'll have forgotten about it. He'll probably tell her he's thinking about choosing a biography of Aristotle or something for a future Books & Brews and that'll be the end of it." She smiled, clearly imagining her reaction. "He's so perfect for her."

"They're perfect for each other," he agreed.

Seconds ticked away in silence, and then her expression turned serious. "Since your computer's better, do you want to go ahead and upload that while I finish in the kitchen?"

"Sure, I can scan it with my phone and submit it to the lawyer, and then it'll be done."

She nodded, and he watched her walk away before picking up the paper. Once he submitted it, they'd be one step closer to an annulment.

Like it never happened, he thought, frowning at the document. He wasn't so sure about that. He was starting to think being married to Chelsea wouldn't be quite that forgettable.

Chapter Twelve

The following afternoon, after the café closed, John wasn't sad to see the Thank You for Visiting Stonefield sign fly by as Chelsea drove out of town. They'd taken her car because she said they were—something about gas mileage—and he didn't care enough about driving to argue. By the time they reached her preferred grocery store, he was feeling more relaxed than he had since moving into her house, and he got them a cart while she pulled the grocery list out of her bag.

"I'd suggest we split the list to get through it faster," Chelsea said. "But we don't know each other well enough to make judgment calls on brands or impulse buys, so we should probably stick together."

John didn't have a problem with sticking close

to Chelsea. He did have news he'd been putting off telling her, though. And he should probably tell her *before* they did the shopping.

"So I called Alfred before we left your house," he told her, putting his hand on the cart to stop her.

"You don't look happy about it."

"He said his contractor hasn't even been able to look at the house yet. So that *might take weeks* that I thought might mean ten days to up to two weeks might actually mean *could be enough weeks to be a month*. Like the way parents say a baby is eighteen months old instead of a year and a half."

He was surprised when she laughed, and then she put her hand on his arm. "I'm sorry. I know it's not funny, but it's just really clear you haven't dealt with our local contractors yet."

"I knew the time frame would require some flexibility, but it's been a few days and he hasn't even looked at it yet."

"It's frustrating. But if it makes you feel any better, I *have* worked with our local contractors and that's why I'm buying extra of some of the items on the list, like laundry detergent. I made the offer knowing you'd be using my guest room for longer than ten days to two weeks."

"That does make me feel better," he said. He'd been worried about watching her struggle to maintain a polite but slightly forced expression as she told him that of course, he could stay as long as he needed to. But she sounded as if she honestly didn't mind having him around and the low-key knot in his stomach since he called Alfred loosened.

"Okay," she said, turning her attention back to the list on her phone. "This is a pretty generic list, so add what you need as we go. General stuff, we'll split. Individual stuff, we'll pay for our own. But to save time, we should pay for it all together and then figure it out at home from the receipt."

"Sounds good." He leaned close to see the list. "It's a little light on meats and vegetables."

"I like to buy that stuff at Dearborn's. Not much of a selection, but it's fresher."

It took them over an hour to get everything they needed. He didn't mind. He spent so much time sitting in a desk chair, he didn't mind walking around the store.

"It's nice to shop without the editorial comments," he said while she was running items through the self-checkout and handing them to him to bag.

"What do you mean?"

"I've never gotten out of Dearborn's without hearing somebody's opinion on how I should choose tomatoes. One time I got a lecture on the evils of canned spinach. Look, if it's so bad, maybe don't stock it on your shelves?"

She laughed. "If you think lectures about canned spinach are bad, they keep the boxes of condoms behind the counter. Imagine *that* lecture."

"I like to support local businesses as much as the next guy, but there's something to be said for a delivery truck leaving a plain cardboard box on one's porch." He had to concentrate for a few seconds on opening the next bag because the thin plastic wouldn't separate. "Anyway, it's just one of the many things I miss about living in a city. I like having a certain degree of anonymity."

"Okay, but there are advantages to a small town. Does a big city supermarket put aside the last jar of apricot preserves because it's the only kind I like?"

He stood straight, a bottle of dishwashing liquid in his hand. "Really? Apricot is the *only* kind?"

"Yes." She handed him a box of dryer sheets. "I bet you're a grape jelly guy."

"Are you saying I'm boring?"

"Not boring. Just…more into the tried-and-true."

"Grape jelly is a classic."

"Says a guy who doesn't even like coffee."

He chuckled and went back to bagging because she was still scanning and he could only hold so many items in his hands.

As they loaded the bags into the back of her car, he peeked into the top of each, running through what he'd bagged. "I don't think we bought anything that needs to go directly into the fridge or freezer. Especially since it's cold today, and getting colder by the minute."

"Like I said, I get most of my perishables at Dearborn's. Why?"

"While this city barely qualifies to be called that, it *does* have more dining options than Stonefield. Let's get dinner before we head back. My treat." When she hesitated, he nudged her elbow and grinned. "Come on. There's a place I've been to a couple of times on North Main Street you'd like."

She laughed. "You're really being a snob right now. Not only do I know the place you're talking about, but I've eaten there."

"I don't mean to sound like a snob. I *like* the diner, but they don't have a liquor license. And Sutton's Place can only serve appetizers and accept deliveries from the Stonefield House of Pizza. Sometimes I just want a nice steak dinner with a glass of wine, you know?"

"I do know. And yes, we can go get a nice steak dinner." She opened the driver's side door and then paused to look at him over the top of the car. "I'm not having wine, though."

"Just one glass?"

"Nope. I'm not drinking with you without supervision again, John Fletcher. Last time I was alone with you and alcohol, I woke up naked and married."

He laughed and got in the car, but he really could have lived without the reminder of Chelsea being naked beside him. He already spent too much time thinking about that as it was.

Chelsea had dressed for grocery shopping—jeans, sneakers and a thick pullover hoodie so she wouldn't have to deal with a coat—and not for dining in a restaurant that drew much of its business from the nearby state government offices. There were a lot of white dress shirts and ties in the place. She'd only eaten here once, thanks to the prices, but the food was good and that was all that mattered.

"I'm definitely having steak," John said, once they had menus and glasses of water. "How about you?"

"I'm leaning toward pasta," she said, perusing the offerings. "The diner makes good spaghetti, but that's about it. Molly told me they tried baked macaroni and cheese once, before I moved here, but so many people in town said theirs were better and argued about the right way to make it, they never offered it again."

He looked at her over the top of his menu. "They tried alfredo back…maybe three months ago?"

Chelsea lowered her menu. "You had that?"

"I tried to. I claimed I was full and went from there to Stonefield House of Pizza."

"It was so bad." She laughed, remembering how she'd fought not to recoil when the fettucine Alfredo had been set in front of her. "It tasted like runny coffee creamer and disappointment."

"It did. It was so watery, and it had that cream taste, but whatever it was, it wasn't Alfredo." He chuckled. "They only served it the one night that I know of—"

"Probably because nobody ate it."

"Which means we were both at the diner on the same night."

She smiled, then took a sip of her water as she wondered how often she and John had almost crossed paths since he'd moved to town. Stonefield was small and didn't have many dining or shopping options, so probably quite often. Of course, the times they *had* crossed paths had been fairly disastrous, so it was probably for the best.

"We must have been," she agreed. "But I usually eat dinner on the early side, so I was probably already gone by the time you got there."

"Did you also stop and get a pizza?"

Her face warmed. "No, I ate the Alfredo. Half of it, anyway. Then I asked for a box for the rest."

"You brought it home with you?"

He looked so incredulous, she couldn't help laughing. "I have a really hard time potentially hurting people's feelings, so I ate what I could, and then I threw the leftovers away at home."

"You never minded hurting my feelings," he pointed out.

"You said my coffee sucks."

"No." He shook his head, grinning as he picked up his water glass. "I said *coffee* sucks, in general. Not specifically yours."

She watched his throat work as he swallowed the cold water before jerking her gaze away. Rehashing the mutual animosity between them before tequila got involved wasn't how she wanted to spend this time. Maybe it wasn't a date, but it kind of felt like one, and she was going to enjoy it.

There was a lot she didn't know about him, but every standard question that popped into her head seemed fraught with the possibility of dragging down the mood. Asking about his family might make him ask more about hers, because she couldn't expect him to remember she didn't have a rosy childhood. And they'd talked about his love for restoring photographs.

"Tell me a funny story about you and Bruce as kids," she said. "He's so quiet, I've never really had a real conversation with him."

"He's reserved with other people, but trust me. He's not quiet." She heard the affection for his brother in his voice, and it made her smile. She always wished she'd had a sibling so she wouldn't have been alone in the world, and she was fascinated by the dynamics. "A funny story, huh? Okay, so when we were kids we watched *IT*, that Stephen King movie, you know? I don't remember how old we were, but definitely too young for a horror movie. Have you seen it?"

"No, but I know it's the movie with the clown and the red balloon."

"Then you know enough." He chuckled, the memory warming his eyes. "Somehow, Bruce got his hands on some red balloons."

"Oh no!" Chelsea covered her mouth with one hand.

"Oh yes. He didn't have helium, of course, so he couldn't make them float. But he found tape in the kitchen junk drawer." He paused, tilting his head as his eyebrows drew together. "Wait. You don't have a kitchen junk drawer."

She laughed. "I'm working on it. There are a few bread ties, some AA batteries that may or may not be good, and a flashlight that doesn't work and of course needs AAA batteries in the drawer with the spatula I never use and the Stonefield House of Pizza menu I never read. It's a start. I think it takes years—maybe even a decade—to build a decent kitchen junk drawer."

"I've got a couple of zip ties and a Sharpie I could contribute."

"Perfect. Bonus points if you don't check to make sure the Sharpie still writes before tossing it in the drawer." She waited while he laughed loud enough to distract the diners nearest them. Then she leaned closer. "I want to hear about the red balloons."

"Right. So the first one was in my closet. I opened the closet door and the first thing I saw was a red balloon, floating at my eye level." He sighed. "It was actually taped to one of my shirts, but it looked like it was floating."

"Did you scream?"

"There's a possibility my scream cracked every glass window in the neighborhood. The next day there was one behind the shower curtain. I…uh." He cleared his throat. "Let's just say the fact I was getting into the shower and therefore wasn't wearing clothes saved my mom some wet laundry."

Chelsea pressed her napkin to her mouth, trying to

stifle the laughter, but it didn't help very much. She had to use the cloth to wipe her eyes and get herself under control because the server wanted to take their order. Once he'd ordered his steak and she asked for the fettucine Alfredo with broccoli—and one glass of white wine, but only one—she took a sip of her water. She'd already laughed so much her throat was dry.

"Okay," she said. "How many balloons were there?"

"Five," he said, shaking his head. "My closet and the shower. Then he waited almost a week before putting one under the bed far enough so it was barely visible. A corner-of-the-eye kind of thing. And then there was one in the basement. I was older, so our mom always sent me down to bring up another pack of soda from the pantry shelves. It was behind the soda. And the last one was in my backpack one morning when I unzipped it to put my lunch in."

"And your parents did nothing?" Chelsea asked, not even trying to hide her amusement. Poor young John.

"Boys will be boys," he said in a high-pitched voice that was clearly meant to mimic his mother. "But Dad put a stop to it when he got out of bed in the middle of the night to pee and tripped over me because I'd fallen asleep on the floor in my parents' room with a knitting needle in each hand."

"Who were you going to stab with the knitting needles? Bruce?" Maybe not having siblings wasn't the worst thing that ever happened to her.

"I don't remember going into my parents' room, never mind getting the knitting needles from her basket, but I probably wanted them to pop red balloons." He sighed, shaking his head even though the memories made his eyes warm and the corners of his mouth turn up. "Okay. Now you. What movie really scared you when you were a kid?"

They were still talking about scary movies when their meals arrived, and they only paused the conversation long enough to thank the server. Here, away from everybody and everything, it was so easy to talk to him. He was so much funnier than she ever would have guessed from their prior interactions, and she appreciated how he was able to pull fun stuff from her childhood without stepping into her upbringing and the loss of her parents. Clearly, he'd remembered.

By the time they finished eating, they'd moved on from movies to the music of their childhood, and they had even less in common when it came to their favorite songs than they did their favorite movies. But they teased each other and found a few they had in common. The conversation was so effortless, Chelsea thought if it *was* a date, it wouldn't have felt like a first date. More like a fourth or fifth date.

Not bad, considering they were actually married.

They passed on dessert, but she watched John hesitate—looking at his glass—when the server asked if they'd like more. If he had another glass, she'd be tempted to have a second, as well. They were having such a good time, she really didn't want to leave.

But even after the big meal, she didn't want to drive the back roads home after two glasses. And it might have taken a lot of alcohol to get her into his bed in Las Vegas, but she knew it wouldn't take very much at this point. Or any, she reluctantly admitted to herself. Another glass of wine might make it too easy, though.

"We've got a lot of groceries to put away," she said, and John lifted his gaze from the glass to her. For a few seconds she imagined she could see him giving himself the same talking-to she'd just given herself, and then he told the server he'd just take the check.

Chelsea would have loved to stay for another hour or two. More laughter. More wine. More of his company. And that was dangerous for her peace of mind. The sooner they got back to Stonefield, where everybody was in their business and she couldn't forget this was her husband—not a man she was casually dating—the better.

Once they were ready to leave, John stepped ahead of her so he could hold the door. As she passed by him, he put his other hand on the small of her back. Just for a moment, in what would have been a natural gesture if they were really a couple.

But it made Chelsea's breath catch in her chest,

and even though she knew it wasn't possible, she imagined she could feel the warmth of that touch all the way home.

Chapter Thirteen

Tomorrow's November fifteenth, which means the winter parking ban is in effect until April fifteenth. No vehicles can be parked on the road between the hours of 11 pm and 6 am, and violators may be towed. Chief Bordeaux would like to add the following statement: "It's not up to residents who watch the weather forecast and decide it's not going to snow. It's every night. Period. Come on, people. We do this every single year."

—Stonefield Gazette *Facebook Page*

A few days later Chelsea pulled into Ellen Sutton's driveway and parked behind Molly's car. Since it was *her* party, she probably wouldn't be leaving any time soon.

After getting out of her car, she took a moment to appreciate the big Queen Anne home that was an inn before David and Ellen Sutton bought it. She'd always loved this property, and thought it was the prettiest house in town. The inn had often hosted weddings and events, so there was a large gazebo in the backyard that overlooked the river. And several years ago the family had done a beautiful job of converting the carriage house into Sutton's Place Brewery & Tavern. Having enough land to put the parking for the taproom on the far side of the carriage house, so it was accessed by the other road and not Ellen's driveway, had definitely helped.

She grabbed the gift bag off the passenger seat and Evie met her at the door. "Welcome! We're just waiting for Irish and the boys to sneak out the back door with Leeza and then we'll get started. Jack and Eli are dragging their feet because there's a lot of food in the kitchen."

Chelsea set her gift on the card table they'd set by the door and then greeted everybody. The Sutton women: Ellen, Gwen, Mallory, and Evie. Molly's mother, Amanda, of course. Laura Thompson. It was the small group Molly considered family, and she was glad to have been invited. Sure, she'd been the maid of honor, but she'd also been *at* the wedding. They could have left her off the viewing list.

"Go make yourself a plate," Ellen told her, waving

toward the kitchen. "And leave room for seconds and thirds because we made too much food, as always."

She wasn't kidding. Jack and Eli, whom Irish must have finally gotten out of there, didn't need to worry. They'd be eating leftovers for days. Which reminded her, she wanted to make sure John remembered she wouldn't be home for dinner tonight. After setting her plate down, she pulled out her phone to text him.

Not sure if you remember I won't be home for supper tonight because I'm at Ellen's for Molly's party.

I probably would have remembered when I sat at the kitchen table and there was no food on my plate.

There was a slight pause and then another message followed.

Kidding. I remembered, and I can forage for myself. Although, I've heard tales of the food at Sutton gatherings and you might be able to sneak some out for me.

Chuckling, Chelsea leaned her hip against the counter, plate forgotten. How do you text so fast? It takes you like ten seconds to send a whole paragraph.

As much as I'd like to brag about magic thumbs, my messages come through my computer, so I'm typing on my keyboard.

She smiled at her screen. That's cheating.

Or efficient. But if I have to reply on my phone, the message will either be very short or you'll be waiting awhile.

"Chelsea, are you coming?" she heard Ellen call.

"I'll be right there."

It's time. I'll bring you some leftovers, she sent to John.

Have fun. I'll see you at home.

She stared at the text message for a long moment, and then locked the screen and slid it into her pocket when Ellen called her name again.

Okay, so she knew what he really meant. He would see her at *her* house, which he was temporarily residing in. That would be a ridiculous thing to say. He'd gone for brevity. *I'll see you at home.* Short and to the point.

So why had it made her breath catch and her pulse quicken?

The others were waiting when she walked into the living room, and she squeezed onto the couch next to Molly, who had Amanda on the other side. Her mother had a box of tissues on her lap, just in case. Running a funeral home meant anticipating tears, Chelsea guessed, and Amanda was ready.

Mallory hit the play button and everybody sighed

when the screen faded in and "Elvis" began singing a slightly sketchy rendition of "Can't Help Falling In Love."

"Oh," Amanda said in a small voice when Molly appeared, looking as absolutely stunning as Chelsea remembered.

There were plenty of sniffles and the tissue box was passed around as they all watched Elvis lead Molly and Callan through their vows. Chelsea wasn't crying, though. With every minute the video went on, she got more tense.

She and John had more chemistry on screen than a soap opera leading couple. And all she could do was hope everybody in the room was so busy watching Molly, they didn't notice.

Watching John watch her on the screen, Chelsea remembered the intensity of his look and the heat in his eyes, and the way it was so potent, it was almost a physical touch.

Then the camera caught John looking up the entire length of Chelsea's body before he shifted slightly and ran his finger under his collar, and Mallory paused the video and looked at her.

"Chelsea."

"I don't know if you can blame the tequila anymore," Evie said to her. "I mean, look at you guys sober."

"Honestly, we drank so much, we might not have been totally sober yet."

Laura fanned herself with her hand. "Good Lord, Chelsea. How did you not just burst into flames?"

"The camera's exaggerating it," she mumbled.

Evie giggled. "So instead of adding ten pounds, it added about fifty degrees?"

Mallory hit the button to resume the video, and there were a few more sniffles as the ceremony wrapped. Chelsea held her breath, realizing what was about to happen, and hoping the videographer stopped filming before…

Nope. It was happening.

On the screen, Molly dropped her flowers. John, who had his back to Chelsea, bent to pick them up and—*yes*—she stared at the way the pants pulled tight over his exceptional ass. Her fingers curled into a fist and her chest heaved as she inhaled deeply.

She looked like a woman who'd skipped lunch staring at a pan of baked macaroni and cheese she wasn't allowed to touch.

Chelsea covered her face with her hands as the women around her reacted, and then she waved a hand at the television. "I mean, *look* at him."

"Rewind that," Ellen said, and they all laughed.

And then Mallory did, and they all watched John bend over again. And then one more time before Chelsea got up and tried to snatch the remote from Mallory's hand. Mallory was quick, though, and she wasn't giving it up.

"I think we're all losing sight of what's really important here," Amanda said, and they all sobered, prepared to be chastised for taking the attention off the bride. It was her daughter's wedding, after all. She leaned forward, looking past Molly to Chelsea. "Is he *really* sleeping in your guest room?"

Laughter broke out, and she put her hands on her hips. "Yes, he is sleeping in my guest room."

"Are *you* sleeping in your guest room?" Evie asked.

"No." She wasn't supposed to be the center of attention here—the bride was. But Molly was laughing with the others, and clearly having a great time at Chelsea's expense.

Gwen, who had her hand rested on her stomach even though her pregnancy was barely starting to show, sighed dramatically. "That seems like a wasted opportunity."

"Opportunity to what?" Chelsea demanded, and then she held up her hands when they all laughed. "Stop! He's sleeping in my guest room, I'm sleeping in my own bed and, in case you all forgot, we're going through the legal process of *not* being tied together."

"Seems like you could have a little fun while you wait for the annulment," Ellen said, and there was more laughter.

"Mom!" Gwen threw a balled up napkin at her.

"Just sayin'."

Chelsea laughed along with the others, though it sounded slightly forced to her own ears. Over the past week, having a little fun while they waited for the annulment was a thought that had crossed her mind approximately nine thousand times, at all hours of the day and night.

The awkwardness had faded between them and they'd become, at the very least, amicable roommates. But it felt more like a genuine friendship—just one with a higher risk of spontaneous combustion due to unsatisfied sexual need than most.

It *had* been a long time since she'd satisfied that need…sober, anyway. And it would be easy enough to get together, seeing as how he lived in her house. She'd been trying to keep those thoughts at bay, albeit unsuccessfully, by reminding herself that John had only wanted her because of the tequila.

But—despite what she'd said—he'd definitely been sober during Molly's ceremony and judging by that video, she'd been very wrong about that.

John walked into the taproom of Sutton's Place Brewery & Tavern and pulled up a seat at the bar. When he got the text message from Bruce telling him it was beer o'clock, he realized it had been several weeks, at least, since they'd gotten together after work.

The bartender, Irish, was a cowboy from Montana who'd rolled into town to visit his old friend Lane Thompson, fell in love with and married Mallory Sutton. John didn't know the whole story, but he'd heard Irish's family situation had been rocky, so he'd taken his wife and stepsons' last name after the wedding. Then he'd bought into the brewery business and Irish Sutton could be found behind the bar most nights.

"What'll you have?" The cowboy set a coaster in front of him. "I hear tequila's your drink of choice, but we don't have a license for that."

John laughed, remembering how he'd sworn off alcohol after waking up with a wicked headache and a wife. He knew it wouldn't stick, but at the very least he could minimize the chances he'd make a mistake like that again. "I'll be dealing with the repercussions of that tequila for a while, so something that doesn't pack too much of a punch would be good."

Irish nodded. "Lane and I brewed up a low-ABV spiced ale for the holidays. Might be just the thing."

"Sounds good."

His glass—etched with the brewery's logo of three lupines—was almost half-gone when Bruce finally arrived. His brother ordered a stout and then Irish moved to the other end of the bar.

"How's the wife?" Bruce asked, and John snorted. "Oh, come on. My oh-so-responsible older brother got wasted and married his least favorite person in town. No way can I leave that alone."

"You know, I've heard you have a reputation in this town for not talking much. Have they even met you?"

"Not the annoying younger brother version of me." He took a long draw off the beer. "But seriously, how's all that going?"

"We've spent more time doing paperwork and more money than we'd like, but it's a process. Pretty sure we've jumped through all the hoops at this point, so hopefully the annulment will come through soon. And they'll finish repairing my house and I'll move back in. Then it'll all be behind me."

"Is that what you really want?"

John barked out a laugh. What was with the people in his life lately thinking he and Chelsea had something real going on? "What are you talking about?"

"You seem different since you went to Vegas. More relaxed and almost happy somehow, which is kind of the opposite of what I'd expect."

"And you're basing this on a few phone calls and running into each other at the gas station the other day?"

"Yup."

"I am *not* more relaxed or somehow almost happy." As if the stress of his situation wasn't enough, he was living with a woman he craved and couldn't touch. He was anything *but* relaxed.

"Don't forget I've known you my entire life," Bruce said, and John rolled his eyes. "And you like that woman."

John didn't want to talk about his feelings for Chelsea. They were messy and complicated, and he couldn't even make sense of them himself. He certainly wouldn't be able to coherently verbalize them, even for his brother.

"How are the girls?" he asked, changing the subject.

Bruce snorted, but he allowed the change in topic—

probably because his daughters were his favorite thing to talk about. He caught John up on all things Jenny and Carrie, including Jenny already talking about wanting a smartphone because all of her friends have one. Ann-Marie had asked their daughter if all her friends jumped off a bridge, would she jump, too, and then she'd locked herself in the bathroom and cried because she'd turned into *her* mother. Jenny still wasn't getting a smartphone, though.

He also talked about work a little bit. He'd worked for D&T Tree Service for years, running the crew that took care of their contracts with the utility companies to keep the trees trimmed back from power lines. There wasn't much to say about work, though. Bruce had a strong sense of keeping work and home as separate as possible, so he kept his mouth shut and did his job.

John figured that must be why he had a reputation for not saying much around town. He'd been shocked the first time he heard that because of the two of them, Bruce was actually the talkative one. In fact, he did most of the talking as they made their way through a second beer and a basket of nachos.

John had his eye on the clock, though, and eventually he took out his wallet and paid the bill. "You told Ann-Marie you'd be home in time to say goodnight to the girls and I'm beat."

It wasn't entirely true, but he *was* in a hurry to get home. He and Bruce parted ways in the parking lot and he drove just a *little* bit over the speed limit on his way back to Chelsea's house. He made it within a few minutes and after taking off his shoes and coat, he headed straight for the couch.

Where Chelsea was sitting.

She looked surprised to see him. "I thought you'd be out until much later."

It wasn't until she tugged the fleece throw a little higher that he realized she'd already changed into her pajamas. The top was well-worn flannel in a Henley style, not lacy lingerie, so he wasn't sure why she seemed self-conscious.

"I'm always home by eight on Wednesdays. I never miss—" He broke off because she was in her pj's, on the couch, remote in hand. And she owned the television.

"Was the fill-in-the-blank there *Survivor*, by any chance?"

"Yeah."

Her face brightened and she shifted to make room on the couch. "Get a drink or a snack if you want. Five minutes until it starts."

It took him six, but he ran to the kitchen, started the Keurig to brew a hot chocolate K-Cup, sprinted up the stairs to change into flannel sleep pants and an old Celtics sweatshirt, and then ran back into the kitchen to get his hot chocolate. He was slightly out of breath when he set his mug on the side table, but her easy laughter made it worth it.

When he sat on the other end of the couch, she even pulled the excess blanket from under her legs and tossed it over him. He snuggled under it, even though the grin she gave him generated more than enough heat.

"You must be why last week's episode didn't show as new when I got home from Books & Brews, and I had to go find it," she said. "You watched it while I was at the taproom."

"I did. I didn't know you watched it—or stayed up for it—or I would have waited."

"Between Books & Brews and Survivor, Wednesday's my late night, so to speak. It's going to be so fun to watch it with another fan. I never have anybody to talk to while it's on."

And talk they did. It didn't surprise John at all they had different favorite players, but as far as he was concerned, that just added to the fun. They talked strategy, drank hot chocolate and—during commercials—shared some of their favorite players and challenges from previous seasons.

They also argued about which one of them would last the longest on the show.

"I'd play a great social game, I think," she said. "But what skills do you have that would keep you from getting voted off the island?"

He put his hand over his heart, feigning offense. Or mostly feigning. Did she think he had *no* skills? "I could play a social game. I can also start a fire and Bruce and I used to fish all the time. Food providers stick around for a while."

"I'd probably beat you in the challenges. There's always a balance beam and I have excellent balance."

He shrugged. "There are more puzzles than balance beams, and connecting visual pieces is a big part of what I do. I admit you'd be better socially, though. We'd do better working together."

"We could be in an alliance together." She shrugged, grinning, and then threw a throw pillow at him. "Right up until I voted you off."

He ducked the pillow easily, and then laughed at the sound she made when it almost knocked his hot chocolate mug off the table. Then the show returned from commercial and it was time for the tribal council.

"He's going home," she said about one of his favorite players.

"No chance."

When his player did, in fact, get voted out, Chelsea wasn't shy about laughing at him. "I told you I'd be better at this than you are. You wouldn't even see it coming—total blindside."

"Nah. I'd flirt with you and you'd vote the way I told you and give me your immunity necklace to keep me there with you."

This time the throw pillow hit him in the face and she laughed so hard, she almost fell off the couch. He picked the pillow up off the floor and lobbed it back at her, but she batted it away.

"How many of those things do you have?" he asked, which just made her laugh harder.

Then they both reached for the throw pillow at the same time and ended up in a tangle of arms and legs on the floor.

Chapter Fourteen

We've regretfully closed the comments on our cranberry sauce poll. We had no idea people held such strong opinions about whole berry versus jellied cranberry sauce, or that the members of this community would take the opinions of others so personally. Dearborn's Market assures us they have sufficient amounts of both varieties, so all of you can enjoy your cranberry sauce just the way you like it this holiday season.

—Stonefield Gazette *Facebook Page*

Even though she was laughing harder than she could remember laughing in a long time, Chelsea felt a thrill at the weight of John's body on hers. He'd managed to get his arm under her head so it didn't hit the floor, and one of his legs was wedged between hers.

It was reflex that had her arms wrapped around him so her hands were on his back. That was what she told herself, anyway.

Their amusement faded, but he didn't move. He looked into her eyes and she could feel his muscles tremble with the effort to keep from full, whole-body contact. She was drowning in his eyes, and he wanted to kiss her. It was written all over his face and in the way his gaze kept flicking to her mouth, but he wouldn't lower his lips to hers without an invitation.

She knew she only had seconds to make up her mind. Any second, he was going to push himself to his feet and the moment would be lost. But if she cupped the back of his neck and hauled his mouth to hers, there was a good chance he was going to end up in her bed again.

And this time she wouldn't be able to blame the tequila.

She didn't care. Before the inner voice in charge of reason could pipe up, Chelsea withdrew her hand from above his waist and cupped the back of his neck.

It was all the invitation he needed and they met halfway. She lifted her head as she lowered his and their mouths collided. The kiss effectively silenced that common-sense voice and she shifted her hand up until her fingers slid into his hair.

They kissed until she was breathless. His body

was heavy on hers, and his thigh pressed between hers. One of his arms was still trapped under her head, but the other was free and it skimmed down her side until his fingertips gripped her hips.

When they finally came up for air, he grinned down at her, the tops of his cheeks brushed with pink. "I might be too old to do this on the floor."

When she laughed, he rested his forehead against hers. "I hope you don't need help getting up."

"I've got this," he said.

And he did, though he winced slightly. Then he reached down and took her hand to help her up. It would have been a lot easier for her to just roll over and push herself up, but he was trying to be chivalrous so she let him haul her to her feet.

It was worth the effort when they were standing face to face, close enough to kiss again. His hands were on her arms and she tilted her head back so she could see his eyes. The hunger there took her breath away.

"Do you know what really sucks about that night in Vegas?" he asked in a rough voice.

"More than waking up married to the woman who got your car towed?"

He chuckled, a deep and throaty sound that made her want to arch her body against his. His hands on her arms weren't enough anymore. She wanted to feel them *everywhere*.

"Maybe even more than that," he confirmed. "I

hate that I had you in my bed and don't remember every single second of it."

The constant ache for his touch flared into a hunger she couldn't resist anymore, and she stepped closer. His hands slid up her arms to her shoulders as she moved, one continuing up to cup the back of her neck.

"Just to be clear," she said. "I had *you* in *my* bed."

"Your room was closer to the elevator. I probably couldn't wait until the end of the hall."

Chelsea ran her fingertip down his throat to the dip below his Adam's apple. "Sounds like you were pretty hot for a woman you didn't like very much."

"As I recall that feeling was mutual. You told Laura Thompson you would duct tape your knees together before you let me in there."

"One, you weren't supposed to hear that, obviously. And, two, I was drinking coffee when I said that. I was drinking tequila when I forgot it."

"You're sober now."

"Yes, I am. And so are you, so there's no reason to deny what we both want. No strings. No interfering with our lives. Just enjoying each other's company while we're living under the same roof, and then we'll go our separate ways. As friends."

"Yes," he said, his gaze so intense, she shivered. "If you're sure."

And she was done talking about it, so she nodded. Then she slid her fingers through his, locking their hands together, and led him toward the stairs.

Chelsea ignored the part of her brain telling her

this was a very bad idea. Maybe it was, but the two of them living together in a near-constant state of denied arousal wasn't much better.

And she didn't have to worry about where it would lead because it was a dead-end road. John was going to leave Stonefield when his leases were up, so there was no future to think about. There was only right now.

Once they were in her room and he let go of her hand to strip his shirt off and toss it away, that voice in her brain stopped talking and her phone slipped out of her grasp and bounced on the carpet. She ran her hands over his chest and down his arms, reveling in the feel of his naked skin under her palms.

He tangled his fingers in her hair, pulling her close for a kiss that seared every nerve ending in her body. His tongue slid between her lips and she opened her mouth to him, surrendering completely.

His other hand cupped her breast, his thumb making hard circles over her nipple. The sensation through the thin fabric of her sleep shirt made her moan against his lips, and his fingers tightened in her hair in response.

But she didn't want that barrier between his touch and her skin anymore. Shifting away from him, it took her seconds to toss the shirt aside, and then peel her sleep pants and underwear down enough to step out of them.

Heat flared in John's eyes and he undid the button of his jeans. As he lowered them, his phone fell from his back pocket. As lost in the moment as she was, Chelsea knew stepping on their phones would kill the mood.

She swept them both up off the floor and carried them to the nightstand while he stripped the rest of his clothing off. After setting her phone on the charger and his next to it, she opened the nightstand drawer and pulled a condom out of the box she'd bought recently. It went next to the phones and then John's arms were around her.

From the corner of her eye, she saw him throw back the covers and then he cupped both of her breasts, his mouth on her neck. Pressing her hands down on the nightstand, she pushed back against him and he moaned, which delighted her. She rocked harder, pressing against his erection.

Then he was spinning her around and she gave a startled laugh when he picked her up and dropped her onto the mattress. She started to shift backward to give him room, but he tucked his hands behind her knees and dragged her back to the edge.

Standing between her knees, he bent and caught her nipple in his mouth, sucking hard enough to make her gasp. Her nails bit into his shoulders as he did the same to her other nipple before kissing his way down her stomach. When he lifted her hips so he could close his mouth over her, she bunched the sheet in her fists, closing her eyes.

John took his time, moving his mouth and hands

over every part of her until she pounded her fist on the top of his shoulder.

"Please. I need you, John."

His weight shifted and then he was gone. She heard the crinkling of the condom wrapper and shifted so her head was properly on the pillow so his legs wouldn't hang off the side of the bed.

When he lowered his body over hers, she caught his face in her hands and lifted her head to kiss him. He nipped at her lower lip as he guided his erection into her. A sigh escaped her and she would have closed her eyes, but their gazes locked and he grinned as he filled her completely.

"This is even better sober."

"Yes," she breathed, and then he started moving his hips.

Then there was nothing but pleasure. The friction. His hands on her flesh. The heat of his skin under her fingertips. Their breath mingling as he kissed her. The hoarse sound of her name on his lips as he thrust faster and harder.

The orgasm shook her, and she dug her fingertips into the flexing muscles of his back as her back arched. His breath was ragged and she'd barely caught her breath when his hips jerked and he groaned as he found his release.

John collapsed on top of her, kissing her hair and her jaw before dropping his head on the pillow next to hers. She wrapped her arms around him, holding him close as their bodies trembled in the aftermath.

"I've been wanting you like this since… I guess it must have been since the red dress," he murmured against her ear. "This was even better than I'd hoped."

"Or remembered," she said, and his chuckle shook her body.

He kissed her shoulder then rolled to the edge of the bed. But as she pulled the covers over herself, he didn't get up. "I'll go turn the lights off and lock up. Did you already set up the coffee for the morning?"

"Yeah." She snuggled deeper under the covers, but he still hadn't moved. She realized he might be unsure about whether or not he was coming back to *her* bed, especially since her alarm would go off at a ridiculous hour. She didn't care. "Hurry back. It's cold without you and I'll need you to warm me up again."

When John woke, the room was still dark and he was alone. Chelsea's side of the bed was cold and he didn't hear her moving around the house.

He reached out to where he'd tossed his phone on the nightstand to touch the screen and bring up the clock. Ten minutes until his alarm would go off. There was no sense in going back to sleep, so he spent those ten minutes thinking about last night.

They shouldn't have slept together, and also he really wanted to do it again.

He'd been savoring the fragmented memories of their night together in Las Vegas, but last night had been even better. While they'd probably made a messy situation even messier and the smart thing

to do would be retreating back to their separate bedrooms, he had no regrets.

After taking care of the clothing scattered around
the floor, he took a shower and then made Chelsea's
bed. Then he went into his room and plugged his
phone in to charge while he got dressed.

When the phone chimed, his pulse quickened
and he grabbed it, anticipating seeing a text message from Chelsea that would give him some idea of
how they were going to handle what had happened
last night. But it was from Callan.

I found that book yesterday that we talked about.
The photo-heavy history of the town that was ru-
mored to exist does in fact exist. It's in rough shape,
but I think some of the photos will help you restore
the ones you're working on for us.

Usually, a client finding an old book containing
pictures he could work from in restoring a few heav-
ily aged and damaged photographs would excite him,
but not after thinking it might be Chelsea.

I'll stop by when you open and take a look at it.

See you then.

It didn't make sense to go into the office just to
leave it again when the library opened, so he burned
some time and anxious energy doing housework.

Chelsea had already picked up the throw pillows and straightened the living room, so he gave the half bath downstairs a good scrubbing. When it was time he locked up after himself and drove straight to the library.

He had to wait for a couple of early-bird patrons to finish at the circulation desk, but then he and Callan were alone to look over the *very* old book unearthed in the bottom of a trunk in the cellar.

"There have been some issues with the preservation of historical volumes," Callan said, the frustration clear in his voice. "But luckily, this one's in good shape. It has several pictures of the old main street you should be able to work from."

When he turned to one of them, John nodded. "I can work with that."

"Obviously, this one isn't in circulation, but since it's probably been in that trunk for decades, I don't think anybody will notice if I let you take it with you." When John just nodded again, Callan tilted his head. "You okay? You usually get a little more animated about old pictures."

"I'm animated on the inside," he said with a chuckle. "Just have a lot going on right now."

"How's that going? We have room if being at Chelsea's is too much, and I don't want to hear any of that honeymoon period stuff. Yes, Molly and I are newlyweds, but we've lived together for a while and we'll be taking a trip to New York City in the spring.

Right now our life isn't very much different than it was before we went to Las Vegas."

"I can't say the same, that's for damn sure."

That was an understatement. Before they went to Las Vegas, he was a divorced man living a quiet life who was focused on his business and reconnecting with his family. Occasionally, there would be some conflict with this business's neighbor, but other than that, his life was on an even keel.

Now he was a married man who'd moved in with his wife and—last night—had slept with her for the second time. And since they'd both felt the first time was a mistake best blamed on alcohol, he wasn't sure where she stood on the matter now. He wasn't even sure where *he* stood, honestly.

"I mean it, John. We can put a bed and a clothing rack from Ellen's secondhand shop in one of the upstairs rooms by the end of the day."

"I appreciate it, but... I'm really okay." John concentrated on *looking* really *okay*, though he wasn't sure how it translated. "Chelsea and I are getting along fine."

He was tempted to confide in Callan just *how* fine. They were friends, after all. He'd been best man at his wedding. But he had to go with the assumption anything John told him would be shared with Molly and he had no idea if Chelsea was going to tell her friend or not. And while he felt like it would be natural for him to confide in a friend, he wouldn't make that decision for Chelsea—especially since she probably cared more about being the subject of gossip in the community than he did since she was going to live here for many years.

When another patron walked in, two young children in tow, John took the opportunity to escape the conversation. He picked up the book. "I appreciate this. I'll take good care of it and get it back to you as soon as I'm finished with it."

"The offer stands," Callan said.

John nodded and then walked out into the chilly, overcast day. It was the kind of raw day that promised snow soon. They'd had a few dustings and one storm that dropped several inches, but they'd melted the next day. It wouldn't be long before the real snow came, though, and it wouldn't leave until spring. It wasn't one of his favorite things about Kansas City and he'd known it would be even worse in New England, but it was worth it to be close to Jenny and Carrie.

John managed to sit in his office for almost an hour before he couldn't take it anymore. Chelsea hadn't called or sent him a text message and he had no way of knowing if it was because she usually didn't, or if she was also struggling with what last night meant for them—assuming it meant anything to her at all. No strings, just having fun while they were sharing a house, she'd said.

Waiting until he got back to the house after work didn't seem like the best course of action. For one thing, that would mean a long day of thinking about the situation while he should be working. And for another, it might be even more awkward. If he walked in the door and kissed her hello and it was an overstep, she might be upset. If he walked in the door and didn't, she might be upset. He couldn't sit with that all day.

What he needed was one of those London Fog lattes she made.

After locking his office, he walked the few steps to the café and pushed the door open. The bell rang and when she turned to greet him, her smile faltered. For a few awkward seconds he thought about walking backward, pulling the door closed behind him and hoping she'd forget he was there at all.

Then her smile widened, her eyes warm, and he stepped all the way in. There were several women at a table in the back, but they were deep in conversation and didn't even look up. Since they were all talking over each other in a way that suggested they'd all asked for added espresso shots this morning, he didn't think they'd be eavesdropping.

"It's chilly today," he said. "I've been sitting over there thinking about that tea you made for me."

It wasn't entirely accurate, but he still didn't have a feel for how they were going to be with each other. He wanted to take his cues from her, but she was in barista mode and giving him nothing.

"One London Fog latte coming up."

It wasn't a fast drink to make and he didn't want to just lean against the counter and stare at her while she worked. Actually, he did, but he wasn't going to. Taking his phone out of his pocket, he looked for notifications and had none. Checked his email, but there were no new ones. Then he checked the weather app and it was going to be cold and there would be some flurries, but nothing big.

When she set it on the counter, he took out his wallet and once she'd rung it up, put his card in the reader. Once he'd put it away, there didn't seem to be anything else he could do but thank her and pick up his drink.

But she put her hand on his wrist when he reached for it, and when she spoke, it was in a voice barely above a whisper. "John, I don't regret last night—I *really* don't regret it—but I don't know if we should do it again. Things are so complicated and I don't want to make it worse."

She didn't regret it. Relief swept over him and, even though he'd be sorry not to share her bed again, her thoughts seemed to align with his. It was amazing and they weren't sorry, but they probably shouldn't do it again. "We're on the same page, then."

Chelsea looked as relieved as he felt. "Okay. So I'll see you tonight then, and we'll probably have soup and sandwiches since I was a little distracted this morning and forgot to throw the roast in the slow cooker."

"Who makes roast at four in the morning?"

"Clearly not me," she said with a laugh. "I'll make it tomorrow, though, since… I won't be distracted."

"Or if you do forget, you can tell me and I'll start it."

"I won't forget," she said firmly, and he heard the deeper meaning there.

It was time to let it go. "Thanks for the latte. I'll see you later."

Once he was back at his desk, sipping the hot beverage, he felt better. At least he knew where he stood and now he could get on with his work.

But he couldn't help feeling a little disappointed. For better or worse, he really would have liked to distract her again.

Chapter Fifteen

*The joy of giving season is almost upon us!
You'll be seeing Santa Fund tags going up in
our local businesses soon, each with the age
and wish list of a child who'd love to have gifts
under their tree this year. While the tags are
being made, you can always make a cash do-
nation through the town's website or at town
hall, and our volunteer elves will do the shopping for you.*

—Stonefield Gazette *Facebook Page*

The next day Chelsea was wishing she'd posted a *sorry,
closed for the day* message on her social media and
stayed in bed.

It was slow. *Very* slow. She knew it was due in part

to there being six days until Thanksgiving. Big grocery bills meant people were less inclined to treat themselves. And there was a cold drizzle that wanted to be snow, but couldn't quite manage to turn over. But knowing why it was slow didn't make the day go by any faster.

It also gave her plenty of time to think about John. They'd been okay last night over soup and sandwiches, and they'd cleaned the kitchen together before settling into the living room where she'd read while he watched reruns of an old sitcom. But the awareness they were each thinking about having sex and were trying really hard not to was obvious.

If Alfred didn't get John's house ready to move back into very soon, their tumbling back into bed together again was almost inevitable.

When the bell over the door finally rang, Chelsea put down the cleanser she'd been scouring her sink with and turned to see Evie walk in with Gwen right behind her. "Good morning."

Three steps in, Gwen froze—distress creeping into her expression—and then she shook her head. "Nope."

When she turned around and walked out, Evie sighed. "I told her this wasn't a good idea."

Chelsea busied her hands wiping down a counter that didn't need wiping because she didn't want to give anything way if Evie asked how things were going with John. "Was that a 'nope, it's not a good morning' or a 'nope, can't be in here specifically'?"

"The smell of coffee is making her sick right now.

As is the smell of meat cooking and the lingering scent of chain saw oil."

"Poor Case." While it would be worth it to have a baby in the long run, Gwen's husband loved coffee and steak, and he made his living with a chain saw.

"Yeah. How are things with you?"

"Good." Chelsea looked over at the tables to see if any needed wiping, and then wondered if one of her ceiling lights was flickering. "Things are good."

Evie was moving her head funny, as if she was looking for something, and Chelsea laughed. "What are you doing?"

"I'm trying to get you to make eye contact with me." She slapped her hand down on the counter so hard, Chelsea jumped. "*You* had sex with your husband."

"Shh," she hissed, even though there was nobody else in the café. "And you all need to stop calling him my husband."

"You mean the man you're legally married to?"

"Only until they get around to signing off on the annulment. I don't want it to be a habit you all have trouble breaking."

"Does Molly know?"

"That we're waiting on our annulment and that I wish you'd all stop calling him my husband? Yes, she does."

Evie snorted. "No, that you had sex with him."

"I didn't say I did."

"You also haven't said you didn't. And I wouldn't

believe you, anyway." She leaned forward, grinning. "So does Molly know?"

Chelsea thought about denying it, but she'd never been good at poker, and Evie definitely wouldn't believe her. "Nobody knows."

"I think when you're somebody's maid of honor, you're supposed to share details like that. And I know. And I'll have to tell Gwen and Mallory. It's a sister thing."

"Sure, and then maybe somebody could come write it on my window in huge chalk paint letters."

"That seems excessive, but it would probably be good for business."

Chelsea laughed, Las Vegas popping into her head again. "I'm pretty good at hashtags."

They were still laughing when Gwen walked back in. She had more color in her cheeks now, and after inhaling deeply, she let out the breath and smiled.

"Okay. I think it's safe." She still had a hand pressed to her stomach, though. "What's so funny?"

"Chelsea had sex with her husband."

"Evie! He's not my—" She stopped, rolling her eyes. "We're not calling him that."

"Can you get an annulment if you've consummated the marriage?" Gwen asked, tilting her head.

"They consummated it in Vegas," Evie reminded her.

"Also, it's not the nineteenth century," Chelsea said, though she actually didn't know the answer. It wasn't on the form, so she assumed it was a nonfactor in this day and age. "We were too intoxicated to understand and consent to a *legal marriage*, so it's just a formality. It would have been easier to take care of it the next day, while we were still there, but Molly thought it would be bad luck on her wedding day."

"She told us she made you wear the rings all day," Gwen said, and Chelsea nodded with a sigh. "But back to you re-consummating your marriage. Everybody who watched that video knew it was going to happen. I mean, you and John might actually be the only two people who didn't see it coming."

The door flew open and Molly rushed in, slightly out of breath and with cheeks flushed with exertion. "I made it!"

Chelsea looked at Evie. "Did you seriously text her to come over here?"

Evie held up her hand. "No, I did not."

"I was at the bank and saw them walking this way." Molly looked back and forth between them. "Why would she text me and, if she had, why would that be bad? What's going on?"

As far as Chelsea was concerned, they could all have this conversation without her because she had nothing to say, so she waved at Evie to go on since she seemed to like telling people.

Of course, once Molly knew, it would only be a matter of time before Callan knew, and she wasn't sure how John was going to feel about that. There was no reining the women in, though, so she hoped he was getting used to how the Stonefield gossip mill worked.

As if he needed another excuse to want to leave this town in his rearview mirror.

"I knew it," Molly said, bouncing on her toes. "All you needed was a romantic weekend in a beautiful place to realize you actually like each other."

"*Like* might not be a strong enough word," Evie suggested, and Chelsea shook her head. This was getting out of hand.

"Um, no. Let's not be throwing the word *romantic* around like that. We have chemistry and we're getting along, but let's not make more out of it than that." She crossed her arms. "And maybe we don't need everybody in town to know?"

"Mallory," Evie and Molly said at the same time.

"I won't be able to not tell Mal," Molly continued. "But that's it. I'll *try* not to tell Callan, but maybe John told him. I can drop hints and see if he already knows."

Molly dropping *hints* meant if Callan didn't already know, he would soon, but none of this was in Chelsea's control so she wasn't going to worry about it.

"I have to pee," Gwen said. "I thought that wouldn't kick in for a few more months."

"You haven't gone since I picked you up," Evie said. "It's not like you're peeing an unusual amount."

"The restroom's for paying customers," Chelsea said, though she was mostly joking. "And so far none of you have ordered a thing."

* * *

It was later than usual when John walked into the house, thanks to a brutal game of Chutes & Ladders with Jenny and Carrie. It was a game that seemed to take forever, and he'd actually been trying to think of ways to cheat when Jenny finally claimed victory.

Chelsea was headed toward the stairs with a basket of folded laundry—and he did his best not to notice the lace bra on top of the pile—but she set it down to carry up later when she saw him.

"I put the leftovers in the fridge, so you can heat them up if you haven't eaten," she said.

When he'd sent her a message saying he'd be late because he was stopping by to see the girls, she asked if he'd be eating with them. He wasn't sure, but told her not to wait for him. "Thanks. I had some chicken nuggets and fries, which is one of the best things about having young children in the family."

She laughed. "Add them to the list for our next shopping trip. Grown-ups can have chicken nuggets whenever they want. One of the benefits of being an adult."

Our next shopping trip. The words stuck in his mind. She probably meant the next trip to Dearborn's because she couldn't possibly mean the once-a-month trip to Concord. Or maybe she could since they were in limbo. No annulment decree yet. No updates from Alfred's contractor other than he was working on it.

Every day he was here with Chelsea, the more it felt like real life. Like the house he'd been renting was in the past and now he was here. They'd go shopping and wash dishes together and it would just go on that way indefinitely. It wasn't an unpleasant thought, but having a plan would be nice.

But speaking of plans, he was reminded of his conversation with Ann-Marie, and he followed Chelsea into the kitchen.

"Do you, uh…do you have plans for Thanksgiving? Like with Molly and her family?"

"No. Molly ends up eating with her family and then going to Ellen Sutton's to have pie and stuff with all of them. I'll probably sleep in until at least five and then spend the day in my pajamas."

"Five, huh? Sounds decadent." He cleared his throat. "But Ann-Marie says it would be unforgivably rude for me to show up for Thanksgiving dinner at their house without my wife."

She shook her head slowly. "I'm not your wife."

"Okay, but technically you *are*, and Ann-Marie says I can't come to dinner without you." He shrugged. "You can probably go in your pajamas."

"Your sister-in-law is literally holding Thanksgiving dinner hostage and the ransom is us showing up and pretending we're married?"

"Again, we *are* married and—"

"You're being really adamant about us *actually* being husband and wife right now," she pointed out.

"She makes this dish with sweet potatoes and marshmallow and, yes, I know everybody has that for Thanksgiving, but the way she makes it is incredible. I think it's the brown sugar."

"Everybody uses brown sugar in it, John."

"Okay, so maybe it's not the brown sugar. Maybe it's something else. The point is I'm asking you to go to their house for Thanksgiving with me so I can have the sweet potato and marshmallow dish."

She was wavering. He could see it, and he chose to give her a moment to process it rather than pushing.

It probably wasn't a great idea. They were already blurring boundaries while playing house, and spending the day as a "family" wasn't going to help.

"How much of this game your sister-in-law is playing involves the girls?" she asked. "Ann-Marie brings Jenny and Carrie into the café sometimes and I don't want any *Aunt Chelsea* nonsense happening."

"I brought that up because I don't want that, either, and she said the girls know nothing and it will stay that way. You'd just be a friend joining us for dinner." He grinned. "Trust me. Ann-Marie's cooking is worth it."

"What are we bringing?"

"What do you mean?" He'd been around enough married couples to recognize the look she gave him. She sure looked like an actual wife in that moment. "I don't know. She said she already has everything, so there's nothing for me to bring except you."

"I'm not showing up at somebody's home for Thanksgiving empty-handed."

"I can ask her again."

"And she'll say *nothing* again." She sighed and put her hands on her hips.

"I'll take care of it. I'll go into Concord and get a nice bottle of wine and…something else."

"Fine." She pointed at him. "But those sweet potatoes better be exceptional."

Chapter Sixteen

*Happy Thanksgiving, Stonefield! We hope you
have a wonderful day with a lot of laughter, too
much food and just the right amount of family.
Chief Bordeaux and Chief Nelson have asked
us to remind you there's a light wintry mix in
the forecast for tonight, so plan your travel ac-
cordingly and don't drink and drive. As always,
our police and fire departments will be watching over the community, but they'd be thankful
for a quiet day. Enjoy that turkey, folks!*

—Stonefield Gazette *Facebook Page*

"Uncle John!"

Chelsea watched the two little girls race each other
to be the first to get a hug. Jenny was older at eight,

but six-year-old Carrie had long legs and determination. It was a tie and John caught a girl in each arm, holding them close.

She tried to ignore that *aww* pang in her heart. John triggered enough pangs in other parts of her body on a regular basis. She definitely didn't need her heart getting in on the act.

"Thanks for coming," Bruce said, giving Chelsea a tight smile.

He was a hard one to read. She knew he had a reputation for being quiet, so maybe he was shy. The few times he'd been in the café, that had certainly seemed to be the case. Or maybe he wasn't happy his wife had insisted John bring Chelsea to the family dinner.

"Thank you for inviting me," she said, returning the smile while holding up the basket she'd taken from John when she saw his nieces coming. "We brought wine and some pastries."

"Ann-Marie's in the kitchen. I can take those back for you, if you want."

"I can take them back and say hello, and you guys can talk."

"That would be great, actually. I'm trying to get the tablet set up so the girls can FaceTime with my mom. They usually use Ann-Marie's phone, but she has some recipes on it and my phone's made to be rugged, not smart, so we're on Plan B."

"I can help with that," John said.

Chelsea left the men to the girls and tech and followed the delicious aroma of roasting turkey to the kitchen. Ann-Marie smiled when she walked in, and she put down her knife to peek into the basket.

"John picked up a bottle of wine," Chelsea said. "And he said you had enough food for today, so I brought you some apple cinnamon rolls with maple butter icing for breakfast tomorrow."

"Oh, are those Alma's? They're delicious and the last thing I'm going to want to do in the morning is cook breakfast, so thank you." She lifted out the bottle of wine, scowling at the label. "John always brings wine. It must be the city in him because we'd rather he just stop by the taproom and pick up a crowler of beer."

"He does seem to miss living in a city," Chelsea said, feeling the increasingly familiar ache in her chest every time she thought about him moving away. Maybe her heart was already a little more involved than she was willing to admit. "What can I do to help?"

"I think everything's under control. You can pull up a stool and catch me up on things, though."

She couldn't really say no, so Chelsea pulled one of the island stools out and sat. "Alfred still doesn't have a date on when the repairs will be done."

"Yeah, Bruce drove by yesterday and he said work's being done, but not quickly. And the holiday weekend won't help, of course. What about the annulment?"

Chelsea blew out a frustrated breath. "We should have been issued the decree by now, but we're still waiting. I told John I'll try to follow up on Monday and see what's holding it up."

"Legal stuff's the worst. We appreciate you letting him stay with you, even with the unique circumstances. We would have made room for him, of course, because he's family, but it would have been hard for everybody—especially the girls. I'm not sure any of us would have survived them sharing a room."

"The man cooks and cleans," Chelsea said. "I'm going to miss him when the repairs are done and he goes back to cooking and cleaning in his own house."

"Maybe I *should* have made room for him to crash here," Ann-Marie said, and they both laughed.

There'd been a truth bomb in Chelsea's words that she didn't want to dwell on too much, though. She *would* miss him, and it wasn't going to be about his willingness to do his share around the house without being prodded. She enjoyed his company and after moving here and before Vegas, she'd been alone but not lonely.

Being welcomed into Stonefield and making friends—especially Molly and the Sutton sisters—had given her that sense of community she'd craved her entire life. And she'd gotten to know many of her customers beyond how they liked their coffee. She built her business. She worked around her house. Her life was full and she'd been content. Sure, she was going to feel a desire to share it with somebody someday, but that hadn't happened yet.

Then she went to Las Vegas for one weekend and everything changed. When John left, she was afraid that she wouldn't be content being alone anymore, and that loneliness was going to kick in with a vengeance.

To expel those depressing thoughts, she asked about Jenny and Carrie. As expected, Ann-Marie was happy to talk about her daughters and she chatted away while she worked. Chelsea took over some of the prep work and there was a lot of sampling.

Ann-Marie swallowed the pepperoni and cheese she'd popped into her mouth, and then nodded toward the snack tray. "Can you bring that to the table before I eat so much of it I don't have room for turkey?"

"Good idea."

She carried the tray into the dining room and then decided to detour to the bathroom. She could hear a woman's voice trying to get a word in around the girls' excited chatter, so they must have gotten the tablet figured out. Or they could be using John's phone.

She must have walked through the camera's field of vision, though, because she heard John's mother ask who she was.

"That's Chelsea. Uncle John brought her with him because he lives with her now."

"Really?" John's mother said, drawing out the word so it was clear to Chelsea she was reading a lot more into Jenny's words than she should be. *Reeeeee-ally:* "Where is your uncle right now?"

Chelsea figured she had two options. She could yank the power plug from the back of the router and kill the FaceTime call, or she could disappear and let John worry about getting out of explaining their situation to his mother in front of his nieces.

She didn't know where the router was, so she kept going and locked herself in the guest bathroom. Jenny was yelling for John, and Chelsea hoped she found him soon. Hiding in the bathroom wasn't a good long-term strategy.

But she didn't want to hear what John said to his mom. It wasn't that big a deal, really. He'd probably just explain that she was a friend and, after his house was damaged by a small fire, he's staying with her until it was fixed. All very reasonable, and nothing that should get his mother too excited.

There was no good reason to be avoiding it, except for the possibility that listening to him dismiss their relationship as nothing might hurt. It made no sense. But as she looked at her reflection in the mirror, she couldn't deny the truth.

Their relationship wasn't *nothing* to her anymore, and she was afraid anybody looking at her while John minimized things between them would see the truth.

She was debating on climbing out the window and walking home when somebody knocked lightly on the door. It didn't seem as if enough time had passed for it to be John. She didn't have any experience with FaceTiming a parent, but his mom was going to have a *lot* of questions.

Pretending she wasn't in there and the door had mysteriously locked itself was out of the question. And she wasn't sure she'd actually fit through the window, so she opened the door to find Ann-Marie sitting on the other side.

"Are you okay?"

Chelsea decided her best option was the truth. "I'm hiding."

"Oh, good." Ann-Marie's relief was evident. "I was afraid my food made you sick and the turkey's not even out of the oven yet."

"Jenny was on FaceTime and told his mom that John brought me because we live together now."

"Ouch. He'll have fun explaining that, so I don't blame you for disappearing. But you should come hide in the kitchen with me. There are no snacks in the bathroom."

Luckily, they could get to the kitchen without being seen by John or the camera, but Chelsea could still hear his mother's voice. She couldn't make out what she was saying, though, and Chelsea didn't know her so she couldn't judge her tone. Ann-Marie just raised an eyebrow and shrugged.

It was almost ten minutes before John walked in, scrubbing his hands over his face. "Well, that was fun."

"It's not that complicated if you leave your recent trip out of it," Ann-Marie said. "You had a small fire and you're staying with a friend while they repair the damage."

"That would have worked, if Jenny hadn't told Mom her name. She's aware Chelsea and I…haven't exactly been friends in the past."

Chelsea snorted. "You complained about me to your mother?"

"*Complained* is a strong word. In passing, I may have mentioned some of our past difficulties, though."

"Past difficulties?"

"You did have my car towed. And there was the spilled, sticky mess in front of my door."

"I didn't spill that." She pointed her finger at him. "And you got my business closed down entirely for days while they did an electrical upgrade we didn't need because you claimed my equipment made your lights dim."

"They definitely dimmed."

The oven timer went off and Ann-Marie muttered something about being saved by the bell under her breath. "Okay it's about to get serious in here. John, go find your brother and make sure he's keeping an eye on the girls. Chelsea, how do you feel about mashing potatoes?"

Smashing lumps out of potatoes sounded like a good way to exorcise her annoyance with John before they all sat down to eat. She waited while Ann-Marie took the turkey out to rest and then, once she had everything she needed, she started the process. Using the electric hand mixer she was given wasn't as satisfying as doing it manually, but there was still something comforting about the process. As she added milk, butter and pepper, her flare of irritation faded.

She couldn't be mad at John for complaining about her. She'd certainly done her share of venting about him. If that adage about your ears burning if somebody was talking about you was true, he probably thought he suffered from a weird, recurring fever.

"Admit it—I was right about the sweet potatoes and marshmallow thing." John took his eyes off the road long enough to glance at Chelsea, but she was staring at the windshield. He could see the curve of her lips, though, before turning his attention back to the road. "Come on. Admit it."

"Fine, I admit it. The entire dinner was better than I've had in years." She snorted. "Especially last year."

"Where did you go last year?"

"Nowhere. I stayed home and had a turkey sandwich. But I also ate an entire can of cranberry sauce by myself, so that was festive."

John had also eaten alone, though he'd bought one of those prepackaged heat-and-serve dinners from a restaurant. But it was that holiday season—the void between Thanksgiving and Christmas—when he'd started thinking seriously about moving to Stonefield.

"I'm glad she sent us home with leftovers," he said. "We get to have it again tomorrow night."

"They need to get out here and start taking care of the roads," she said when he slid a little at a stop sign.

"We're almost there. I'm glad we didn't travel farther than Bruce's house, though." He was able to get into the driveway with no problem, but he could see that it would be slippery. "I'll help you get in and then come back for the leftovers."

She laughed. "How do you think I got in and out of my car in the winter before you were here?"

"I know, but I'm here now and it would seriously ruin Thanksgiving if you fell, so humor me, please."

She did, waiting until he'd gotten out and made his way around the car before she opened her door and got out. It wasn't as bad as he'd feared, but he stuck close to her as they started toward the porch.

Suddenly, she slipped and, to keep from falling, clutched his arm. He turned and slid his other arm around her, holding her up. His footing wasn't much better, so they were still for a moment, getting their bearings.

The scramble not to fall had brought Chelsea into his arms, and John wasn't inclined to let go of her any time soon. Yes, it was cold and there was a mix of snow and sleet falling on their heads, but it was worth it.

After a long moment she tried moving her feet and one slipped, so she clutched him tighter. He couldn't help it—he wrapped his arms around her and buried his face in her cold, snow-covered hair.

He wasn't sure when her grip went from trying not to fall to returning his embrace, but the side of her face rested against his coat and for a few moments they just held each other in the driveway.

Then she tilted her head back so he could see her face. Her gaze lingered on his mouth before their eyes met. A snowflake landed on her lashes and she blinked, smiling, and he was powerless to stop himself from kissing her.

Chelsea didn't pull back. She relaxed into his embrace with a low hum of pleasure that seemed to vibrate through his entire body. He dipped his tongue between her lips and she opened her mouth to him.

He never wanted to stop kissing her, but then she shivered and he couldn't be sure if it was desire or the fact they were standing outside in the cold with winter precipitation falling on them. After nipping once at her bottom lip, he pulled back with a sigh.

"We made it a week and a day," she said softly. "I'm surprised we lasted that long."

"It wasn't easy," he confessed. "We need to get you inside now. Carefully, and hopefully without landing on our butts."

Doing a kind of penguin shuffle side by side, with their fingers threaded together, they made it to the porch. He let go of her hand and had her go first up the slippery steps. He wouldn't have enough traction to keep her from falling, but he'd at least be able to keep her from hitting her head.

Once she was safely across the threshold, he took the time to scoop some of the salt and sand mixture she kept in a bucket in the corner of the porch and scattered it over the steps. Then he went back for another scoop and made his way back to the car. After getting the tote with the leftovers, he got back to the porch without falling and tossed some more of the mixture in as wide an arc as he could manage. There was very little chance anybody was going to stop by in this weather, but just in case.

Chelsea was in the kitchen, humming a Christmas song and prepping the coffeemaker to go off at dark o'clock tomorrow morning. After stowing the leftovers in the fridge, he put the tote back in the pantry and stepped up behind her.

He lifted her hair and kissed the back of her neck. When she shivered, leaning back against him, he smiled. They'd only been together twice, but he was learning all the places she got off on being touched or kissed. Every shiver—every sigh—thrilled him and when he wasn't touching her, he was thinking about it. He craved the feel of her skin under his hands and mouth.

He knew he should at least *try* to rein himself in. This was all going to come to an end at some point, though, so all he could do was try to get his fill of her now. Maybe if he could somehow sate his hunger, it would be easier to let her go when the time came.

She pressed her ass against his erection. "How can you even be *thinking* about that after all the food you ate today?"

"I think about it pretty much all the time," he confessed. Then he reached around and cupped her breast, chuckling when his fingers brushed over her taut nipple. "Funny that you're thinking about it, too, considering you had seconds on that pumpkin pie. With extra whipped cream both times, I might add."

"I was trying *not* to think about sex by drowning myself in sweet calories. Obviously, it didn't work."

He slid the hand not cupping her breast down her arm until he could rub circles in her palm with his thumb—another touch that made her shiver. "Maybe we should go upstairs and work off some of those calories."

Her head dropped back against his shoulder when she laughed. "How very predictable of you."

Since her neck was exposed, he lowered his head and nipped at her jaw. "Is that a no?"

"That was a lot of calories. You really think you're up to that kind of workout?"

"Challenge accepted."

He tugged her hand and led her through the house, picking up their cell phones and turning off lights as they went. It was less sexy than hauling her straight up the stairs, but neither of them was going to want to go back downstairs after. And her alarm went off at four, and she'd be dealing with customers before he was even out of bed.

When they finally reached her bedroom, he managed to wait patiently until she'd put the phones down, but then he pulled her into his arms and kissed her with all the passion that had been building up since the last time he had his hands on her.

He didn't see how he would ever get enough of this woman, he thought as he slowly stripped her clothes from her body. He touched every bit of flesh as it was revealed, his hands and mouth savoring the feel of her skin.

His own clothes were discarded in a rush, kicked into a pile. They fell onto the mattress together and he kissed her again as her hands roamed over him. When he drew her nipple into his mouth, she gripped his shoulders and he smiled against her breast.

Only when he'd brought her to her first orgasm with his mouth and his fingers did he grab the condom wrapper she'd pulled out of the drawer. As he rolled it on, he tried to regain control of himself, but he was running low on self-control.

He took her hard and fast, reveling in the feel of her fingernails on his back as she gasped his name. Only once she'd come again, her hips bucking against his, did he let himself go.

And as he lay there, panting against her neck as she wrapped her arms around him and held him close, John knew his immediate hunger was sated, but his need for her was only growing stronger.

Chapter Seventeen

It's Black Friday! If you come across any deals today, share them in the comments. And to fuel your bargain hunting, Chelsea at the Perkin' Up Café is taking 20% off every order today! Grab some caffeine to go and put a dent in that Christmas list. Happy shopping, Stonefield!
—Stonefield Gazette *Facebook Page*

"Stay."

Chelsea smiled when John muttered the word against her shoulder. She was warm and liked the weight of his arm across her body. She only earned money when the café was open, though, and today was going to be brutal. She needed to get a jump on it.

"I can't." She reached her arm out from under the

covers to turn off her alarm and then kissed his cheek. "Today's one of my busiest days of the year. Go back to sleep."

He caught her wrist before she could slide out of bed. "Five more minutes."

"If I give you five minutes, you'll take an hour and I'll have a line of customers waiting to get their coffee so they can shop longer before they drop."

He started shoving back the covers. "I'll go put down more salt and sand."

"It's fine." She pushed his hand away and pulled the covers back over his shoulder. "It warmed up overnight and the driveway's clear. Seriously, go back to sleep."

She let him pull her in for one kiss, though, before she freed herself and went to get ready.

She peeked in before leaving without turning on the light, but she could hear his soft snoring from the doorway. Smiling, she tiptoed away because he could get at least another hour's sleep, if not more.

By the time she flipped the sign to Closed what felt like a hundred hours later, she was exhausted. It was worth it because her sales on Black Friday were always phenomenal, but her feet hurt and he didn't know it yet, but John was doing all the reheating of the leftovers tonight.

When she got home, she toed off her sneakers with a sigh of relief and then went to the kitchen for a glass of water. She drained half of it and then refilled it before going out to the living room. Sink-ing onto the couch with a sigh, she set her drink on the end table and unlocked her phone. Some mindless surfing was just what she needed, but she'd start with her email.

When John walked through the front door, she was still sitting on the couch, but she wasn't relaxed. She was sitting on the edge of the seat feeling utterly wrung out after a flurry of emails and one very long phone call.

She stood when she heard the door and watched him take off his shoes. "Have you checked your email in the last hour?"

He froze in the act of tossing his keys onto the table. "No. Why?"

She took a deep breath and told herself to just say it because there was no way to soften the blow. "Our annulment was denied."

"What?" He let go of the keys and they fell on the floor. "I don't understand."

"They denied our annulment."

"No, I heard the words. I just don't understand why they're coming out of your mouth. We were too drunk to consent to the marriage."

"We were sober enough to convince the officiant we could consent. And thanks to Alfred's house bursting into flames and the affidavit having to list where you were served, our paperwork has the same address, which means it's obvious to the powers that be we're living together." She shook her head. "And, as a joke, Molly changed my outgoing email name to *Mrs. Chelsea Fletcher* and then forgot to tell me about it, though I don't know how the judge saw that, unless the lawyer just forwarded stuff. Or maybe he uploads things to a server? I don't know how it all works. I just know it was denied."

"Is this a prank? Because it's not funny at all."

"People who get super drunk and get married and then regret it the next day don't continue living as man and wife."

"We're not."

They actually kind of were, but she knew what he meant. "On paper, we look like we are."

He took a few steps toward her, accidentally kicking his keys under the couch in the process. She knew she should say something because he wasn't going to be able to find them in the morning, but his gaze was locked on hers and she couldn't look away.

"Did you explain to them what happened?" he demanded. "Is there somebody we can call? A way to appeal?"

"I did call, and the lawyer said it's done and we need to jump through all the hoops for divorce proceedings. And then I tried to call the court clerk because, honestly, the lawyer should have caught that stuff, but I didn't get anywhere."

He blew out a breath, shoving his hand through his hair. "This can't be happening."

Chelsea couldn't believe it, either, but the lawyer had assured her at least a dozen times that, yes, the standard for annulment was actually very high and not granted as easily or often as people thought. Of course, when they'd hired him, he'd assured them it would be quick and easy, so she didn't know what to believe at this point. Except the fact they were legally married and would be remaining so until they were granted a divorce.

She could see John's shock giving way to anger, but one thing she was *not* going to do was take the blame for this. They'd downed tequila shots together, gotten married together, and together they'd decided to temporarily live under the same roof.

"What the hell are we going to do?" He scrubbed his hand over his face and then shook his head. "I'm sorry. I'm not… I just don't know what we do next."

"We take a breath and then we figure out how to get divorced."

"Take a breath," he repeated. And then he tried that, taking a deep breath that she could see did little to calm him.

"It doesn't really change anything," she insisted. "I mean, yeah, it's going to cost us more money, but we'll still make what happened in Vegas go away."

"It hits differently. I know it doesn't make sense, but making it so it never happened and ending it in divorce—a *second* one for me, by the way—are two different things."

"I know. We messed up, though, so this is what we have to do."

After tilting his head back to stare at the ceiling

for a long moment, he exhaled slowly and looked at her. "Are *you* okay?"

Chelsea managed a shaky smile for him. "I've known a little longer than you, so I have a head start on processing it."

"Yeah, but you also had to deal with calling the lawyer and asking all the questions."

"There will be plenty of paperwork for us to do together," she pointed out.

He nodded. "Okay, but I saw the traffic going in and out of the café today and you must be exhausted, so I'll take care of supper tonight. And yes, I know it's just reheating leftovers, but you sit and I'll call you when it's done."

Is this a sign?

John couldn't believe that question kept running through his head. He didn't believe in that kind of thing—signs and portents and all that. But as he transferred the reheated dishes onto the table he'd set, he couldn't stop wondering if their annulment being denied meant something.

It sure seemed like it might. Two people who didn't know each other very well—and didn't like what little they *did* know—had ended up all the way on the other side of the country in a wedding chapel together. And then a random fire had moved him into her house. And now their attempt at being unmarried had been denied. It sure seemed like the universe wanted them to be together.

But he *really* didn't buy into stuff like that, so he just needed to get his head on straight.

Before telling Chelsea the food was ready, he took out his phone and sent a quick text message to his brother. Any chance it's beer o'clock tonight?

The reply from Bruce came through when he was halfway to the living room. Can't make any promises, but I'll try.

"Food's ready," he told Chelsea, slipping the phone back into his pocket.

They ate in silence, for the most part. They'd spent the past three weeks assuming they'd get a document saying their marriage never happened and then life would go on. It had never occurred to him their petition might be denied, and he didn't think she'd had doubts, either.

"I'm going to go out with Bruce tonight," he said when they were almost done. Whether his brother could make it or not, he wanted to get out of the house. And then he fibbed a little because he didn't want Chelsea thinking he was trying to get away from her because he was upset. "He had the girls all day while Ann-Marie bargain hunted and he needs a break."

"I think I'm going to go to bed even earlier than usual tonight," she said. "It was a very long day for multiple reasons and I'm ready for it to be over."

He'd also kept her up late last night, which he'd felt bad about while watching the customer flow outside his window today. He didn't mention it, though, because the vibe in the room felt off, and he didn't think it was the right time to bring up the renewed intimacy between them.

"I'll be quiet when I get back, so I don't wake you," he said, and she nodded.

Back in his own bed tonight, he thought as they cleaned up. They put Ann-Marie's washed and dried containers into the tote to be returned. He'd toss it in his car and if his brother showed, he'd give it to him tonight. Then he told her to get some rest and headed for Sutton's Place.

He got a text message from Bruce right after he parked. Leaving soon. I'll be there.

It was busy, but most of the customers were grouped at tables and there was plenty of room at the bar. He took a stool at the quiet end and waited for Irish to finish ringing up a couple at the register.

"You alone tonight?" he asked, putting a coaster in front of John.

"Bruce hasn't left the house yet, but he says he's coming. I didn't realize until I got here that I should have checked to see if you were open."

"The first Thanksgiving they were open, the family closed for the entire weekend because they'd been up against the wall for months. But financially, it makes more sense to be open." Irish dropped another coaster on the counter, which was as close to a reservation as one got in the taproom. "How was your Thanksgiving?"

"It was…good. How about yours?"

Irish gave him one of the grins that were rare, but lit up the man's face. "Excellent. I'm thankful every single day for this family, and for Mallory and my sons and my baby girl, but you throw in a meal like they pull together and it's damn near Heaven on earth, my friend."

John laughed. "Yeah, my sister-in-law's dinner puts takeout Thanksgiving to shame. And getting to spend the time with my nieces was the icing on the cake."

"And Chelsea?"

John tried not to react when Irish said her name, but he wasn't sure he hid it. "She went with me to Bruce and Ann-Marie's."

"Everything going okay there?"

John sighed. "That's a question that's going to require some of that spiced ale of yours. Actually, it requires something a lot stiffer than that, but I'm driving, so I'll take a spiced ale."

"Coming right up."

After delivering a glass of the ale, Irish did the circuit, checking to make sure none of the other customers needed anything before returning to John. "How's the beer?"

"As excellent as I remember."

"Good to hear. It took off a little more than we expected, so I'm just hoping we can keep it on tap until we close for Christmas. I told Lane customers might try to storm the cellar when we run out."

"That glass wall? I think we could take it."

Irish chuckled. "So how about that answer? How are things with you and Chelsea?"

John hesitated, but the news wasn't going to be a secret for long, and he needed to talk about it. "Nevada denied our petition for annulment today."

The cowboy's eyes widened under his black hat. "I don't think anybody expected that."

"We definitely didn't." He sighed and took a long swallow of the beer.

"So are you here tonight because you're upset your annulment was denied, or because you're not upset about it and don't know what to make of that?"

John arched an eyebrow, surprised his face had given *that* much away. "I think I'm here because I don't know."

"There's no reason you *have* to know, is there?" Irish tilted his head. "Doesn't seem like you need to make an immediate decision on how you feel about it."

"We'll be starting the divorce process. Probably Monday."

"Still, just because you start the process doesn't mean you don't have time to figure out how you feel about it. Or her." Irish paused, but John didn't say anything. He probably shouldn't bare his soul to Mallory's husband—Mallory, who was best friends with Molly, who was one of Chelsea's closest friends. "I'm the bartender. What's said to me in this taproom *stays* in this taproom."

"It's complicated."

"It always is."

"If we'd gotten to know each other without the trip to Vegas, and if I wanted to stay in Stonefield forever or she was willing to leave, I'd be seriously thinking Chelsea is the one." Sweat prickled on John's forehead. He'd admitted it out loud to another person, and he couldn't make Irish forget he'd heard it. It was real now.

"Sounds serious."

He really hoped Irish meant it when he told him what was said in the taproom stayed in the taproom. The whole *what happens in Vegas* thing hadn't worked out so well for him. But he was already in it, so he kept going. "I'd be thinking about the future already."

"Sounds like you already *are* thinking about the future. You just don't think you should be."

"We want different things in life."

Irish looked over John's shoulder. "Your brother's here. Just don't get so focused on wanting different things in life that you don't leave room for the possibility that what you want might change. Trust me on that one."

He nodded at Bruce and then walked away to give them a minute to say hello. His brother sank onto the stool with a weary sigh. "I had to work today because we're behind on a contract, and when I got home I had to play three games of Chutes & Ladders so Ann-Marie could get a break. Three games, John. I love those girls, but that's just too much to ask of a person."

"Hell, you should have told me that. I would have picked you up so you could drink enough to drown the memories in beer."

"I should have." He ordered a spiced ale when Irish came back, though. "I wouldn't mind something stronger, but at least this is good."

"Right there with you."

Bruce looked at him, probably hearing something in his voice. "What's up with you?"

John caught him up on the last episode of the too-strange-for-reality-TV John and Chelsea show. He was expecting shock and maybe a little ranting about the officials in Nevada. Some sympathy would be nice.

Bruce scoffed and waved his hand. "Just stay married."

John barely managed to swallow his beer without doing a spit-take. "What?"

"You like her. We like her. She's got a house already and she makes really great coffee. Just keep her."

"I don't like coffee." It was an inane thing to say, but his brain hadn't caught up with Bruce's conversational blindside yet.

"But you like *her*."

It wasn't a question. "Yeah."

"And she likes you." Also not phrased as a question. "Are you going to get divorced just because you didn't mean to get married?"

That should have been an easy question, but John took a long swallow of beer instead of answering. He didn't know right now, and maybe the best thing he could do was listen to the cowboy bartender.

He didn't have to know right now or make hard decisions today. He'd drink his beer, relax with his brother and then get a good night's sleep. Or he'd lie awake and think about Chelsea, but he'd *try* to sleep. It was all he could do.

Chapter Eighteen

Between gift buying and heating costs, it's an expensive time of year, but that's no excuse for poaching power! Chief Bordeaux reports there's been an increase in complaint calls about residents using poorly camouflaged extension cords to plug into a neighbor's exterior outlet or tapping into their Christmas light strings. While he's been able to mediate amicable outcomes so far, stealing your neighbor's electricity is a crime. If you find a cord plugged in on your property without permission, please report it. Damaging or sabotaging the cord creates a fire hazard and then, according to Chiefs Bordeaux and Nelson, "everybody's going to jail."

—Stonefield Gazette *Facebook Page*

Chelsea was ready when Molly walked through the door of the café on Monday morning. She didn't usually stop in on the weekends and she knew Molly and Callan had gone Christmas shopping in the city, so she'd had to wait to exact her revenge.

She put her hands on her hips when Molly stepped up to the counter. "Do you remember when I had to find out you were dating Callan from Daphne Fiske, but I knew you weren't and I gave you decaf until you told me about your fake dating scheme?"

Molly's eyes widened. "Yes."

"Good. This time you're getting decaf because you changed my outgoing email to Mrs. Chelsea Fletcher and didn't tell me."

She laughed. "Sorry! It was a joke and I meant to tell you, but then I got distracted and forgot."

"Mmm-hmm. It might also be one of the reasons our annulment was denied."

Molly gasped, covering her mouth with her hand. "No."

"Yes. Because Callan served him at his residence, which is my address, and because I'm using Mrs. Fletcher in my email communications, we appear to be living as husband and wife."

"Do you have to stay married forever now?" Molly dropped her hand. "Would that be so bad, though, because—"

"No, we're not staying married forever. But now

we have to go through the time, expense and head-ache of getting a divorce."

Molly's shoulders dropped. "I'm so sorry. I'll have decaf forever. Just plain, with no cream or sugar. Or foam with hearts in it. It was a joke, but I went too far. I always go too far."

Chelsea felt a pang of sympathy. Yes, Molly's actions had complicated things, but she knew her friend felt things more deeply than other people and she'd beat herself up over this for a very long time. "The address—living together—would have been enough. And if not for the annulment, it would have been a funny, harmless prank."

"I didn't think. As usual."

Chelsea laughed and leaned across the counter to pull her friend in for a hug before the tears could start. "It'll be okay. And you don't have to have decaf forever."

"Just today?" Molly pulled back with a sniffle, but Chelsea was relieved the tears were more of a shimmer than an impending waterfall.

She was tempted, but she also knew caffeine was one of the tools Molly used to manage her ADHD and she didn't have the heart to withhold it. "I was kidding, Molly. You can have your caffeine…but no foam art today."

Her face brightened, and then fell again. "Does John hate me?"

"No."

"He probably does. And then Callan will be upset

because if John hates me, they can't be friends anymore and that's awful, because John was his best man and—"

"Molly." Chelsea covered her hand. "John doesn't hate you and you're spinning out. Do you want a hot or iced drink today?"

Offering her a choice between two things she liked worked as a distraction from her emotional distress—Callan had quietly told her about that strategy one day—and Molly looked at the menu board she already knew by heart.

"I have to drive, so I'll just take a large hot coffee with cream and sugar, I think." Molly made a face. "A little boring, but if I get an iced coffee, it'll be gone before I even get to the highway. The hot coffee will last longer because I'll be afraid of burning my mouth."

Chelsea loved her thought processes, and she smiled as she made the drink and set it on the counter. "Not *too* boring."

"Christmas cups!" Molly beamed. "These are so cute!"

The red cups with wreaths were an extra cost, but she knew from last year that they were worth it. Customers loved them. "You have the very first one. I'm not using them until Monday to give Thanksgiving weekend its due, as Mrs. Dyer so vehemently put it."

"Thank you," Molly said, putting her card into the chip reader. "I really am sorry about the email thing."

"It's going to be fine. John and I just seemed to be

trapped in some kind of comedy of errors, but we'll get out of it." Eventually, if the universe would stop sabotaging them.

Molly glanced at the clock and winced. "I hate to run out on you when you have so much going on, but I have an appointment in Manchester and I hate that drive so I dragged my feet this morning and now I'm barely going to make it in time."

"It's fine. We'll catch up soon, and drive safely."

Once Molly was gone, Chelsea started going over her inventory list, but her friend's words kept echoing around in her head.

Do you have to stay married forever now? Would that be so bad, though, because—

Of course it would be bad. They hadn't meant to get married. Before the trip, they didn't even *speak* to each other. There was no way they would have even gone on a first date, never mind walked down an aisle together.

But they had, and then the fire had happened. She'd gotten to know him and that had changed everything.

She was in an emotional danger zone, and she had no idea how to save herself. She'd ignored the warning signs and the caution tape and now all she could do was pump the brakes and hope she could stop herself before she crashed and burned.

We could put the rings back on, cancel the plan to file for divorce and just keep doing what we're doing...forever.

The thought blindsided her multiple times during the morning hours, and it was growing harder to remember all the reasons they couldn't actually do that.

They hadn't ended up together—in matrimony *or* in bed—because they couldn't resist each other. There'd been nothing *but* resistance between them until tequila got involved.

He wasn't living with her by choice. He'd had a fire and she had an extra room and no kids whose schedules would be disrupted by a guest.

And even if those reasons faded into the background, there was the fact John had no intention of making Stonefield his home. That was a big one because Chelsea had no intention of leaving it.

There was a little voice in her head asking if that was still true, though. Maybe being close to his family and having an established business was growing on him. And her. Maybe what they had together was starting to grow on him, too.

She'd been asleep when he returned from the taproom Friday night, but when she saw him Saturday, he seemed more like himself. Clearly, the shock of the annulment rejection was wearing off and it was going to be okay.

She wanted to see him. Maybe it was what Molly had said, or maybe it was just that he was never far from her thoughts, but she decided to make him a London Fog latte and take it next door. He'd mentioned a project deadline that had been moved up, putting him in a time crunch, so he'd probably appreciate the caffeine.

Once it was ready, she looked out the window and didn't see anybody heading in the café's direction, so she put the bell on the counter and carried the drink next door. She wouldn't be able to hear the bell, of course, but she used it mostly to buy herself a couple of minutes. Customers would wait a moment before they rang the bell, and then wait a few more minutes before getting antsy.

John wasn't at his desk, though. She could hear movement in the back and assumed he was either in the storage area or the restroom. Since she couldn't be long, she'd just leave the beverage as a surprise gift.

When she went around the desk to set it down, though, she couldn't help glancing at his computer screen. Just a peek at what he was working on. But it wasn't a graphics program or a photograph on the screen.

It was a real estate site, with the search results for Portsmouth, New Hampshire, showing.

Pained surprise took her breath away and she set the glass down before she spilled tea all over his desk. That answered that, she thought, releasing a long, shaky exhale. John was still planning to leave Stonefield—and her.

"Hey, you," he said, and she forced a smile onto her face before turning to face him. "Who's watching the café?"

"The bell," she said, thankful she was able to get

the words out in an almost steady voice. "I only have a second, but I wanted to bring you a London Fog latte to get you through the rest of the day."

"You're spoiling me," he said, his mouth curving into a smile that didn't reach his eyes. "You okay? You look flustered."

"I'm fine," she lied. "I need to get back, though. I have about thirty seconds after the second bell ring before the customer leaves. Or calls the police to report me missing."

He stepped forward and she didn't know if he intended to kiss her or just sit in his chair, but she moved back around the desk in case it was the former. She wasn't sure she had the strength right now not to throw her arms around his neck and beg him not to go.

His brow furrowed slightly, but he nodded. "I'll see you at home, then?"

Home. "Yeah."

Nobody was ringing the bell when she entered the café, and she was thankful it was empty. One of the harder aspects of her job was smiling and offering great customer service when she wanted to curl up in the storage closet and cry for a while.

She couldn't hide in the closet, of course. But she could take a few minutes to talk some common sense into herself.

He'd never said he'd changed his mind about moving away. They'd made no promises to each other. In fact, the only definitive thing they'd ever said about their relationship was that it was going to end. She'd told him there were no strings. Just like coffee creamer, her time with John had an expiration date. She knew that going in, and she wasn't going to make things awkward by trying to change the terms now.

The bell over the door rang and Chelsea fixed a smile on her face before turning to greet the bank teller who needed three lattes to go.

"I like this one."

John looked at the tree Chelsea was considering. "Are you planning to cut a hole in the living room ceiling?"

"It's not *that* tall."

"It's leaning against the fence." Reaching through the branches, John pulled the tree so it stood straight.

"Okay, it's a *little* tall." She tilted her head. "Definitely too tall. And I don't own many decorations, so it would look naked."

"There's nothing wrong with naked."

She laughed and moved on to the row of shorter trees. He lost sight of her for a moment because the Christmas tree lot was surprisingly busy for a Thursday afternoon, but then he caught up to her. She had her hands on her hips, looking at a tree he suspected would be the one he'd be tying onto the roof of his car.

Coming here had been a good idea. He'd left the office at the same time she closed the café so they could go home and work on the paperwork from their lawyer. It hadn't taken as long as they'd thought it would, but it also wasn't fun and it had put a damper on their moods.

It had been Chelsea's idea to drive out to the tree lot. There was snow in the forecast, so she wanted to buy one before they got covered. She also liked the idea of waking up on the first day of December with Christmas around her, and he felt as if he could use the fresh air and it was a beautiful day—if a little on the chilly side.

He'd almost taken her hand when they got out of the car, but he'd shoved his hands in his pockets instead. It was hard enough making people believe that, no, they were actually not staying married without being spotted holding hands out in public. Just being here together was probably enough to get them going again.

"This one," she said when he reached her side. "This is the one."

"Okay. I'll go find the guy."

As he waited for the lot worker to finish netting a tree for a family, he thought about Monday, when Chelsea had brought him a London Fog latte. She'd been flustered and hadn't seemed like herself, but he'd had too much work to push her for a reason. But even though she'd seemed like herself since then, that moment had stuck in his head and it wasn't until he'd been lying awake in her bed last night—much earlier than he'd normally go to bed—listening to her quiet breathing that it hit him.

The search results for office spaces in Portsmouth had been on his screen when she'd brought him a tea. And because of the work notes he'd had strewn around, she'd had to go around the desk to set the drink down and it would have been human nature to glance at his screen.

And she hadn't said anything. She hadn't asked if he still intended to move away. She hadn't argued why staying in Stonefield near his brother and his family, as well as the business location he'd already established, would be a good idea. And she certainly hadn't told him she didn't want him to go—that she wanted him to stay in town with her.

Maybe if she had, he would have confessed that he'd pulled up the site because he got an email alert about a new potential location, but that he hadn't even bothered to click through the photos. Property moved fast in that area—it had been an ideal location with flow for foot traffic and parking that was certainly better than Stonefield's—but he wasn't prepared to commit to a lease right now. He wasn't sure what he wanted anymore.

"Sir?" The lot attendant waved a hand to get his attention, and John shoved down the thoughts of Monday to focus on the here and now. This was a festive night for Chelsea and he wasn't going to drag the mood down.

By the time they got home and had managed to get the tree untied and off the roof of his car—thankfully, she'd remembered to bring a blanket—it was getting dark. He carried it to the porch and leaned it carefully against the siding. "Do you have the stand? We can set it up out here and let the branches fall for a day or two."

"I know you're supposed to do that, but I don't want to wait. I want to decorate it tonight."

He didn't argue with her. Instead, he waited for her to hold the door open and carried it into the living room. She'd bought a new stand at the tree lot, so he was able to get it set in the corner of the living room where she wanted it. Once the netting was cut away and the branches fell, he carried the two boxes of decorations up from her basement.

"I'll go put something together for supper while you finish this," he told her once he'd helped her wrap two strings of twinkling lights around the tree.

"Let's get a pizza delivered," she said. "I don't want you to miss out on the fun part. We'll eat pizza while we decorate the tree."

It took them ten minutes to decide on toppings— half pepperoni and mushrooms for her and half pepperoni and half sausage for him—and they'd already added candy cane-striped metallic garland to the tree and were rummaging through the boxes for ornament hooks when the delivery arrived.

"If we're going to do this, let's do it right," he said. While she grabbed two paper plates and some napkins, he found a video of a crackling fireplace to fill the television screen, and he found a Christmas playlist on his phone.

Once the small plastic bag of ornament hooks was found, they ate pizza and decorated the tree. Chelsea hummed along with music, and she'd laugh when she hung a heavier ornament on a branch and it would immediately sag. She had a ceramic cat ornament in a red bow that had to sit on one of the stronger branches, and it took her several tries to find a good spot.

"What about the back?" he asked because the tree was definitely not looking symmetrical.

She laughed at him. "Are you going to squeeze back there and stand in the corner to admire the tree?"

"No, but—" He tilted his head, looking at it. "Okay, good point."

"Our tree is perfect the way it is."

Our tree. He liked the sound of that.

His phone rang, cutting off the Christmas song, and he picked it up. Alfred's name flashed on the screen and his stomach sank. "I need to take this."

She picked up the pizza box and the paper plates. "I'll go put the leftover pizza away and we can finish this after."

He knew she was probably assuming it was a client and giving him privacy, and he didn't correct her. Instead, he swallowed hard and accepted the call. "Hi, Alfred."

"John! I have some good news for you. The house is done, for the most part. They need to go in tomorrow and finish cleaning up, but you can move back in on Saturday."

The impact of what his landlord was saying set John back on his heels. The words *you can move back in* came out of the man's mouth, but what he heard was *it's time to leave Chelsea.*

"John?"

"Yeah." He forced himself to focus on the conversation. "That's good news."

"Sorry it took so long."

And yet, somehow, it didn't feel nearly long enough. "No problem. I know how contractors can be. I appreciate you letting me know."

Once he hung up, John tossed his phone back into his pocket and stared at the tree. He'd finish helping her decorate it and then he'd sit and drink hot chocolate with her in the glow of the lights.

But tomorrow was the last day this would be *their* Christmas tree.

Chapter Nineteen

A statement from Chief Bordeaux: "We had our first plowable snow last night, and this morning I received at least half a dozen complaints from residents who found tickets for violating the parking ban on their windshields. Those complaints have been filed in the trash can as I assume they were intended to be notes thanking us for not towing the vehicles despite violating the parking ban. Residents are free to ask to speak to the manager but that would be me, so maybe don't."
—Stonefield Gazette *Facebook Page*

John was gone when Chelsea got home from work. She knew it as soon as she unlocked the door and stepped over the threshold.

The house felt empty.

Three months ago, if you'd told Chelsea she would miss having John Fletcher in her house, she would have laughed so hard she might have peed a little. Just the mention of his name had been enough to raise her blood pressure.

But she already missed him. When he'd told her Thursday night that the house would be done for Saturday, she'd felt as if the bottom had dropped out of her world, and it had taken every bit of self-control she could muster to hide it. The last thing she wanted to do was make him feel bad for getting his life back.

She thought she'd done a good job of it. Yesterday she'd helped him pack up most of his belongings. And this morning, when she'd kissed his cheek goodbye and left him sleeping in her bed, she hadn't cried until she was in her car. Now that she'd gone into her house, though, she didn't want to be there. And there was no sense in taking her boots off until she'd finished cleaning up the end of her driveway. Having a company plow her driveway was a big expense she always questioned, except when it snowed and she had to leave her house before five o'clock. There was always a bit left once the town was done plowing, though, as well as her walkway.

Once that chore was done, she was out of things to distract herself with. And the physical exertion hadn't tired her out enough so she didn't notice the emptiness all over again when she walked through the door a second time. She took her boots off and then took her cell phone out of her coat before hanging it up. There was a text message from Molly.

You doing okay?

No, she was most definitely not doing okay, but talking about it was only going to make her feel worse and not better, so she sent back a thumbs-up emoji and went into the kitchen. That was when she saw the note. It was on the counter, leaning against the coffee brewer, where she'd definitely see it.

Chelsea,
Thank you for letting me stay with you. Your guest room was a lot more comfortable than my brother's couch, I'm sure.
    Even though we got off to a rough start, I'm glad we've spent the past month together. And I'm glad I got to know you. You're an amazing woman and it's going to take a long time to get used to an empty house at the end of the day.
    I know we still have a lot of legal hoops to jump through, so make sure you reach out. I don't want you to deal with the headache alone. And I'll still be stopping by for my fancy tea you got me hooked on.
    Thanks again,
John.

She read it again, the tears flowing over her cheeks by the time she got to the end. It was meant to be a thank-you, but it felt like a goodbye note. And it was her own fault. She hadn't wanted to make things awkward between them, so she hadn't worked up the courage to ask him if he'd rethink his plan to move away. Maybe she would have if he hadn't been searching for Portsmouth properties the day she brought him a tea.

It had been doomed from the start. She knew that. She'd put down roots in this community and she refused to leave. He'd come here with a plan to stay one year and then he was out. Good company and great sex wasn't going to change what they wanted out of life, and she had nobody to blame for forgetting that but herself.

Her phone rang and her breath caught as she pulled it out of her back pocket. But it was Molly again, and she took a deep breath before accepting the call. "Hello, Molly."

"Your thumbs-up emoji is suspect."

"Why?"

"Because if you were really fine, you would have said so. But maybe you're not fine but you didn't want to lie, so you sent a thumbs-up emoji."

Chelsea snorted, turning the note upside down on the counter before going out to the living room, where she collapsed on the couch. "You're overthinking that emoji."

"Are you actually okay?"

"I'm actually okay." Maybe that wasn't totally true, but it would be with a little time. "I'm going to make something to eat and watch TV and then go to bed. Then I'm going to get up and go to work tomorrow. Same as always."

"I don't know if I believe you."

Chelsea laughed, which made her feel better. "I can hear the taproom in the background, Molly. You're supposed to be working."

"Unofficially. They can't fire me for talking on the phone because I don't actually work here."

Because of her friendship with the Suttons, Molly had been involved with the taproom since the beginning and she loved mingling with the customers. But she also hated schedules, so she claimed she wasn't an official employee. Chelsea happened to know that, thanks to things like labor laws and taxes, she actually *was* on the payroll, but everybody let her pretend she wasn't.

"I'm going to go eat now. You get back to unofficially working."

"Fine. I'll talk to you soon."

Once she'd hung up, the silence set in again, though. And Chelsea didn't think turning on the television or some music would dispel it. In the same way a fierce winter wind could chill a body to the bone, without John, silence had settled into the bones of the house.

She wasn't in the mood to cook for one, but her job had her on her feet all day and she needed to eat.

After retrieving her coat and shoving her feet back into her boots, she grabbed her keys and got in her car. Maybe she wouldn't get to eat supper with John tonight, but she didn't need to eat alone.

Saturday had sucked. It shouldn't have since John was back in his own home and would sleep in his own bed for the first time in a month. He should be looking forward to it.

But it didn't feel like home anymore. It was just a house that didn't have Chelsea in it, and that definitely sucked.

The feel of her lips brushing his cheek had awakened him in the early, dark hours, but he hadn't opened his eyes. He didn't want to say goodbye to Chelsea—he didn't even know how to do that—and he hadn't had the certainty or courage to say anything else. He'd just let her go to work as if it was any other day.

He put his hand in his pocket and curled his fingers around the two wedding bands, feeling the gold warm in his fist.

Somehow he'd never gotten around to selling them. He'd put them on the dresser, then at some point he'd set some receipts on top of them. But when he was packing the last of the bits after dragging himself out of Chelsea's bed for the last time, he'd picked up the receipts and there they were. Rather than leaving them or putting them in the pocket of his duffel bag, he'd dropped them in his pocket.

At some point he'd get around to selling them—maybe—but for now he liked being able to touch them. It was strange, but the reminder of his adventure with Chelsea pained him and comforted him at the same time.

"You should get a Christmas tree," Bruce said, yanking him out of his thoughts. His brother had stopped by with the excuse of helping him carry stuff inside, which he didn't need help with, and to see how the repairs turned out.

John knew his brother was right about getting himself a tree, especially since the living room had an empty corner that would be perfect for one, but he wasn't sure he had the heart to go back to the lot and find one for himself.

"Pam got all the decorations in the divorce and I've never gotten around to buying my own. Seems like a lot of work and money for one person."

"We've got so much Christmas crap, I'm sure Ann-Marie could put together a box of decorations for you. Jenny and Carrie could come over and help you decorate it."

John nodded. "Thanks. I'll think about it and reach out if I decide to get one."

Bruce gave him a long look, head tilted. "You okay?"

"Sure." He forced a smile. "Why wouldn't I be?"

"Because you were pretending to be married to the woman you're *actually* married to, which is so messed up, and now the pretending part is over and you're realizing maybe it wasn't so much an act on your part."

"I'll need thirty-six hours and a giant whiteboard to make sense of what you just said."

"Maybe it wouldn't make sense to anybody else, but you know exactly what I'm saying. You let yourself live in a fantasy world for a few weeks and now you're sad the fantasy isn't how everything turned out."

John did know what he was saying, though he didn't want to admit it. On some level, he'd let himself pretend life with Chelsea was real, when it wasn't. But Bruce would see right through anything but the truth. "I don't think she feels the same way."

"Did you ask her?"

"No."

"Then you don't really know how she feels, do you?"

He folded his arms. "I know she thinks I still plan to move to Portsmouth and it didn't matter enough for her to say something about it."

"Okay." His brother scowled. "That's not a great sign."

"She said it was too hard to resist while we were living under the same roof, but then when this place was done, we'd go our separate ways. She didn't say anything when she saw Portsmouth real estate listings on my computer screen. It is what it is, Bruce."

"That doesn't sound good," he admitted with obvious reluctance. "Are you still planning to move?"

He'd been unsure enough so he'd passed on potentially prime real estate, but now he wasn't sure he could stay even if he wanted to. Seeing Chelsea—almost every day since their businesses shared a wall—was going to be painful. "I don't know. Probably."

"You have to do what's right for you, even if I think it's the wrong move. You know Ann-Marie and the girls and I would love for you to stick around."

"I know. I'm not ruling anything out right now. I just need to get my feet back under me, you know?" He gave a humorless chuckle. "And I probably won't go anywhere until my divorce is finalized."

"So you know she saw the listing and assumes you're leaving, but you're not sure. Did it occur to you to tell *her* that?"

"No. She said no strings, and I don't want to pressure her and make things awkward."

"If she said no strings, she wouldn't be upset about you moving to Portsmouth."

"Which is probably why she didn't care enough to say anything," John said. "That's my point."

"This is so messed up, and it's giving me a headache." Bruce shook his head and then slapped him on the shoulder. "I've gotta get home but you know our door's open to you anytime for any reason."

"Thanks for coming over, and give my love to Ann-Marie."

Once his brother was gone and he was alone again, John thought about picking up his phone and sending a message to Chelsea. He could thank her again, but he'd already left a note. There was the snow. He could offer to help, except she'd mentioned at some point she had a plow guy.

No matter what excuse he came up with, he'd only be putting off the inevitable and prolonging the recovery process.

Unable to face cooking dinner for one and eating it alone, either in silence or in front of the television, John grabbed his keys and wallet and left the house.

The diner was busy and as John scanned the dining room, probably looking for a place to sit, his gaze met Chelsea's. Maybe it was his imagination, but for a few seconds she looked really happy to see him.

Maybe the fact he felt the same had shown on *his* face because she smiled and waved him over.

"Do you want to join me?" she asked, and his heart hammered in his chest.

"Would that be weird?"

She snorted. "We got married and then lived together. I doubt dinner's going to raise many eyebrows."

He'd meant *for them*, but he took off his coat and then sat across the booth from her. "Thanks. I didn't realize it would be so busy."

"Word got out smothered meatloaf is on the special board, I guess." She handed him her menu and he took it to give himself something to look at, even though he already knew he was having the Chicken Bacon Ranch wrap. "Now that you're here, I don't have to feel guilty about taking up a whole booth for one person."

"I'd been debating on whether I'd be comfortable doing that, so it worked out well for both of us."

The server stopped for their orders and then brought them each an ice water and mug of decaf coffee. While they fixed their coffees with cream and sugar, he was careful to keep his legs tucked under his half of the table and his hands far enough from hers so their fingers wouldn't brush. He hated that, but focusing on keeping physical boundaries helped keep him from focusing on the emotional pull he felt.

"I got your note," she said. "It was sweet, thank you."

"I meant it."

He'd also meant the first version of the note.

I know you said we were just having fun until the repairs were done, but I don't want this to be the end of us. I think what we have might be the real thing and I'm not sure what the future looks like, but I want us to keep seeing each other while we figure it out.

He'd torn it into tiny pieces and then buried it in her garbage can under coffee grounds. After all they'd gone through, he didn't have the heart to put that kind of pressure on her. She hadn't said anything when she thought he was looking at Portsmouth properties, so he had no reason to believe her feelings on the matter had changed.

"Did you get a Christmas tree yet?" she asked in a cheery voice that sounded fake.

"Not yet. If I do get one, it'll probably be a small artificial one that's prelit."

"Then it won't smell like Christmas, though."

He chuckled. "They make candles for that."

They made small talk while they ate. Jenny and Carrie had given him very extensive Christmas lists, and she laughed when he talked about how Ann-Marie had taken a red marker and scratched out well over half of each list. She told him about a teenager who'd come in with a special Christmas recipe she'd seen on some app, with peppermint and cinnamon and several other holiday flavorings. Chelsea had warned her the combination of flavorings was a bad one, but she'd insisted. When she described how the girl had asked her to video her taking the first foamy sip and Chelsea had gotten about twenty seconds of her gagging before she snatched her phone back, John had laughed until he realized other diners were looking at him.

What they didn't talk about was anything important. She didn't ask him about his future plans. He didn't ask her about hers. Neither of them brought up the divorce. It was as if they both just needed to be in this easy bubble of each other's company for a little while longer.

It lasted until they walked out into the cold night. John could see her car, and it was parked in the opposite direction of his, so this was it. Chelsea was trembling slightly, and he would have chalked it up to the temperature, but she also wouldn't look at him. He was about to turn to her—to ask her if they could get together again and maybe go on a real date—when she spoke.

"We can't do this again," she said in a soft, shaky voice.

"Eat supper?" he joked, not able—or not willing—to wrap his head around the fact he wouldn't even get to share a meal with her again.

She met his gaze then, and there was a finality in her eyes that made his stomach knot. "We knew this would come to an end, when the marriage was dissolved and you went back to your own house. The dissolution might be more complicated than we anticipated, but we're back to our separate lives now. I have plans. You have plans. We need to break the habit of being each other's…company."

She was so much more than that to him. He needed to tell her that—to tell her that his plans were changing and he wanted her to be a part of them. But after giving him a sad smile, she turned and walked away.

And, like a fool, he let her go.

Chapter Twenty

We received word from our librarian that the Books & Brews meeting for tomorrow night has been canceled. Mr. Avery reports that only one person has finished reading the book—it was him, of course—and they'll be discussing it at the January gathering instead. Irish Sutton, our own cowboy bartender and co-host of the event, said it wasn't that it's December, but that the book was boring. As a follow-up comment, Mr. Avery reports the Books & Brews suggestion box was empty last month and he's not taking complaints at this time.

—Stonefield Gazette *Facebook Page*

"Since we don't have Books & Brews tomorrow night, we should do something fun."

Chelsea frowned at Molly. "There's no book club tomorrow night?"

"No. Nobody read the book. I keep telling Callan we want to be entertained, not given an education in the history of…whatever that thing that guy invented was, but he insists it's possible to do both."

She nodded, remembering how she'd gotten about ten pages into the book before giving up because cleaning the grout in the bathroom would be more fun. "It wasn't his best pick."

"And he thinks we're going to discuss it in January, as if an extra month will make it less boring." She leaned across the table. "But I'm going to hijack Books & Brews and pick another book this week and we'll all read *that* one."

Chelsea nodded, but she didn't care. She'd sat at the table with Molly because she needed the distraction, but the cancelation of Books & Brews meant she had nothing to do tomorrow night and would be free to watch the Survivor finale. Under typical circumstances, that would have been a cause for celebration, but now she knew she'd spend tomorrow evening thinking about John and wishing he was there to watch it with her.

It had been over a week since she'd seen him and the loss of him in her days still hurt on an almost physical level. She should have been redoing her window today instead of sitting with Molly, but she couldn't do her window without seeing his. She hadn't plugged her Christmas tree in because the lights made her remember how they'd decorated it together, as if it was *theirs* and not just hers.

"Chelsea."

She snapped her attention back to Molly. "I'm sorry. What?"

"Do you want to do something fun tomorrow night?"

"No." She wasn't going to be good company and she may as well get the show finale over with. "I have plans, actually."

"Oh!" Molly raised her eyebrows. "Plans with your hu…with John, by any chance?"

To Chelsea's dismay, tears welled up in her eyes as she shook her head. "No. There are no more plans with him, Molly."

"No! Oh, Chels. I thought you two were… I thought you were, you know, actually together."

"We were for a while, but you know the story. It was a mistake and then a fling and now it's over." That hurt so much to say out loud.

"Okay, but here me out—what if that night in Las Vegas wasn't a drunken mistake? What if you and John were meant to be?"

Chelsea tried to laugh off Molly's words, but the sound was more like a strangled sob. She settled for shaking her head. She didn't want to rehash what it had felt like to think maybe they had something real, only to find him surfing for Portsmouth properties. She'd had to put an end to their time together so she could stop imagining that he'd change his mind about leaving. Cutting him loose totally was the only way she could start moving on with her life...without him.

She forced herself to smile at Molly. "You're turning into one of those women now—the ones who get married and are blissfully happy, so you want all your friends to do it, too."

"Of course I want you to be blissfully happy. I wouldn't be a very good friend if I didn't."

"The problem isn't that you want me to be happy. It's that you think that will happen with John Fletcher."

"Don't kick me under the table or throw something at me, but you already *were* happy with John."

Molly wasn't wrong, but Chelsea did her best to keep her friend from seeing it. "So I enjoyed having somebody to watch Survivor with for a few weeks. That's a far cry from being blissful newlyweds."

An unusually serious expression settled onto Molly's face and her body quieted, as if the constant current of energy had been dialed down suddenly. "If you don't want to talk about it, I understand. But don't lie to me, or to yourself."

Her breath caught and she pressed her fingertips to her eyes in an unsuccessful attempt to stop the tears. "Fine. I fell in love with him. I started feeling like it was real and that it *was* meant to be, but it's not, Molly. He wants to move away from here—he wants to live in a city—and I don't know if I can do that. All I ever wanted was a community to belong to, with people who know and love me, and I found it here in Stonefield, with all of you. I don't know if I can give up the only thing I ever wanted in my life."

"If he really loves you, he won't ask you to."

"So even though I really love him, I should ask *him* to give up what *he* wants?" She sniffed and grabbed one of Molly's napkins to mop up her face. "And I don't even know if he does. I know he wants me. Physically, I mean. And I know he likes hanging out with me. But he hasn't said anything about not leaving. He was still looking at properties in other places. Maybe I'm the only one who fell for the fantasy. Well, and you, but I need you to stop."

Molly was shaking her head, but Chelsea stood. "A customer might come in any minute, so I can't do this. Can you keep watch while I go wash my face?"

Once she'd locked herself in the restroom, she leaned against the door and forced herself to get hold of her emotions. She was at work, and the people who walked through that door expected a smiling, friendly barista. Though, if she was having a bad day, she knew they'd forgive her for it. They'd rally around her and make sure she was okay. This was her community and her home, and what she'd been looking for.

She loved John, but she couldn't give this up.

Pushing herself away from the door, she scrubbed her face with cold water and cheap paper towels until she felt a little better. And then she looked at herself in the mirror and told herself she was not going to look at her phone.

She wasn't going to see if there were any emails about their divorce. She wasn't going to message John and ask him why he hadn't been in his office this week. If there was something wrong with him, she would have heard through the grapevine. For all she knew, he'd driven over to Portsmouth to check out properties.

She'd told him they needed to break the habit of each other, so she couldn't be upset he'd done just that. All she could do was move on. Run her business, watch her favorite show alone and cook meals for one. Just like she'd been content to do before tequila and a carelessly tossed cigarette brought him into her life.

John figured it was a good thing he'd quoted his client a price for a completed package and wasn't charging him by the hour because he'd been staring at his screen without touching his mouse for so long his hot chocolate had gone cold.

He'd made the drink for the comfort and warmth of it, as well as the sugar and caffeine boost, but the first sip had made him think of Chelsea and once she was in his head, it was hard to get her out.

It had been a week and a half since he'd moved back into his house and they'd ended up at the diner at the same time. The last supper, so to speak. Other than her forwarding some documents from the divorce lawyer she'd found—since neither of them could be sure the previous one hadn't botched their annulment somehow and blamed them—there had been silence between them and he hated it. And the closer they got to Christmas, the worse it got.

He'd just let her walk away. Divorcing her was part of the plan, and he could live with that. Moving back into his own place was hard, but manageable. He could even adjust to not falling asleep next to her. But being cut out of her life entirely? That hurt on a level he hadn't even known existed.

And instead of telling her he wanted them to date—to try to maybe restart their relationship the "right" way—and that he was reconsidering how badly he wanted to live in a city, he'd let her go.

That was what had been tormenting him for the past week and a half. In that moment he'd accepted what she told him instead of telling her how he really felt. Maybe she didn't feel the same. Maybe he'd still be sitting here alone, missing her, but at least he would have tried.

It was almost a relief when the doorbell rang, even though he wasn't expecting anybody.

He was surprised to open the door to find Ann-Marie standing on the other side. His sister-in-law had only dropped by on her own a few times since he'd moved to town, and she always sent a text message first, letting him know she was on her way.

"Everything okay?" he asked because something

being wrong with Bruce was where his mind went first.

"Everything's okay with us, but several people have asked me if you're sick because you haven't been in the office all week."

"It's only Wednesday, so by all week, you mean two days?"

"Sure. So are you sick?"

"No." Heartsick, he supposed, but he wasn't dropping *that* grain of truth into the Stonefield gossip mill. "So I'm working from home. Big deal."

Her eyes narrowed. "When you moved here, you were very adamant you wouldn't be doing that."

Yeah, but when he'd moved here, he hadn't planned on falling in love with the wife he hadn't wanted. And because that wife was also his business neighbor, there was no way to avoid her. Even if he parked on the end of the street that kept him from having to walk by her window, he knew she was there. He could picture her moving around the café, talking with her customers. And maybe it was his imagination, but sometimes he thought he could hear her laughter through the wall.

Over all of last week, he'd probably managed to get a total of a day and a half's worth of work done. Friday morning he'd given up. After making sure all the files he was working with were accessible from his laptop, he'd packed up what he needed and gone home.

He'd go back to the office soon—maybe next week.

The hard edges of missing Chelsea would soften and he'd be able to see her face or hear her laughter without the pain taking his breath away.

"I was adamant I would find balance between work and home," he said. "Having the office space was a big part of that, but it doesn't mean I *can't* work from home at all. Just not all the time."

Her eyes narrowed and he could see she didn't believe him. "Fine, but I'm paying attention. Don't make me worry about you, John. I have enough worrying to do about your brother and the girls."

"I won't." It felt good to have somebody worrying about him.

"Good. And listen, I know you were invited to the Suttons' Christmas party at the taproom on Saturday."

He winced. A holiday party was so far down on the list of things he was in the mood for that he was more likely to scrub the gaskets in his refrigerator door with a toothbrush. "Yes, I was invited, but—"

"You have to go." When he opened his mouth to argue, she held up her hand. "Bruce doesn't like parties, but he was invited because he works for Lane and Case, and he said he'd go if you go. I *really* need a party, John. I need a night out."

He stifled a groan because no matter how much he'd rather grab that toothbrush and start scrubbing, it would be hard to deny Ann-Marie an opportunity to dress up and celebrate the holidays with other adults.

"The last time I got a night out away from the girls was the night I spent in the hospital, getting my gall bladder out," she continued. "We keep talking about getting a sitter and going out for dinner, but we never get around to it. Bruce did take us all out to the diner a few weeks ago, and Jenny knocked over her drink and it got in Carrie's fries and—"

"Okay!" John held up his hands, surrendering totally. "Okay, I'll go to the party. But Bruce better be there."

"He will."

"You know he's going to say you'd have more fun if you make it a girls' night out and he stays home with Jenny and Carrie."

"Oh, he's already brought that up and it's not going to happen. We're having a date night. Period."

He heard the note of finality and yes, Bruce would definitely be going to the Suttons' Christmas party. The smile died on his lips, though, because right on the heels of that thought came another.

Was Chelsea invited? Will she be there?

There was no way he would voice the question to Ann-Marie, though. He didn't want anybody in Stonefield to know he was hiding in his house, pining for Chelsea, even— or maybe especially—his brother and sister-in-law. They'd fuss over him and Ann-Marie might decide to involve herself in the situation, which would leave him not only heartbroken but heartbroken and embarrassed, too.

"I should get back to work," he told her. That screen wasn't going to stare at itself.

"I'll see you Saturday night, then," she said. "And try to get some sleep. You look like hell."

Once she was gone, he saved what little work he'd done and shut his laptop down. It was almost time to wrap it up, anyway, and he wouldn't get anything done by sitting in the chair, looking at the screen and wondering if Chelsea would be at the Christmas party. She was friends with all of the Sutton sisters, and Molly would definitely push for her name to be on the invite list. Molly was practically an honorary Sutton, so that would carry weight.

He could ask Callan. He'd probably know. But he'd also probably tell Molly that John had asked, and she'd jump to conclusions. Probably the correct conclusions, actually, but just like with Ann-Marie, it would invite involvement in an attempt to help.

Instead, he did some housework with a podcast piping directly into his ears with earbuds in an effort to keep his brain from spinning out on him. Then he reheated some leftover stroganoff from the night before. He had never minded eating alone. He did now.

As the clock ticked toward eight o'clock, John felt more and more on edge. He had the text message composed, waiting for him to hit the button that would send it to Chelsea.

Want to come over for the Survivor finale?

What was the worst thing that could happen? She could ignore it and leave him on *read*. Or she could say *no, thanks*. Either of those would be painful.

Or would her showing up at his door be the worst thing? If they spent three hours talking and laughing and bickering through their favorite show, he was going to have a hard time remembering their...whatever it was, was over. And if she also fell back into their old rhythm, they'd end up in his bed. And if it really didn't have any strings for her and was only a matter of chemistry and drive, he'd have to suffer ripping off the Band-Aid all over again.

That would be the worst that could happen.

He watched their favorite show alone, in silence and missing her more than he thought it was possible to miss another person he hadn't even liked two months ago. When the show ended and Chelsea's favorite player got the most votes to win, his phone chimed.

She'd sent him the emoji face wearing the black sunglasses, like a rock star. He sent her back the gold trophy.

And that was it.

Even though they'd clearly been thinking about each other for the past three hours, swapping a couple of emojis was what their relationship was now.

He wanted to call her. Maybe hearing her voice would soothe him enough so he could sleep. But ten o'clock was late for Chelsea to be up—eleven if she stayed up for the after-show reunion stuff—and if she'd wanted to talk to him, she would have called instead of sending the sunglasses dude.

Tomorrow he had to go back into the office. His misery wasn't going to abate and he couldn't hide in his house forever. This was his Chelsea-less life now, and he needed to get on with living it.

When he crawled into his cold, lonely bed, he stared at the ceiling for a while before forcing himself to close his eyes.

Maybe tomorrow he'd miss her less.

Chapter Twenty-One

*The Stonefield Public Library will be closed
today due to a lack of heat. While the return
box is available and services are available online, any materials due today will instead be
due on the day the library reopens. Thanks to
a quick response from Poulin Heating & Air
Conditioning, Mr. Avery hopes that will be tomorrow, but stay tuned!*
　　　　　　　—Stonefield Gazette *Facebook Page*

Chelsea was exhausted on every level. Physically,
she was dragging because the Survivor finale had
been so long and then she'd sent that text message to
John. And *that* meant she'd lain awake, thinking about
him, and wishing he'd been there to watch it with her.

Mentally, her mind was tired of spinning, imagining all the alternative endings their story could have had if things were different—if he wasn't still thinking about moving to Portsmouth. If she'd grown up in a stable family and community situation and felt secure in moving away from Stonefield.

Emotionally, she was just plain beat.

When the bell over the door rang, she turned to greet her customer with the best smile she could muster. It slipped, though, when she locked eyes with Callan. It was a strange time of day for the librarian to stop in, and for a few seconds she was afraid something was wrong with Molly. But he looked too relaxed for that, and she belatedly remembered the heat in the library had failed.

"Hey, Callan," she said. "Molly's not with you?"

"No, she's got a meeting in Manchester with her dad, and she wants to stop at the community college in Concord on the way back to see about taking classes, so she'll be gone all day."

"She told me she was going back to school, and I'm excited for her. Last time we talked about it, she didn't know what she wanted to take classes *for*, but she definitely wanted to do something of her own, rather than being support staff for her parents at the funeral home and the Suttons in the taproom."

He laughed. "Oh, she'll do that, too. She's leaning toward teaching art at the elementary school, and she happened to mention she'd still be able to unofficially work in the taproom some evenings and on weekends."

"Art and kids sounds perfect for her. I can't wait to hear how the college visit goes today."

"I'll let her know that." He took his wallet out. "Can I get a large black coffee?"

Chelsea smiled and headed for the pot. While Molly occasionally talked him into a more adventurous beverage, Callan's favorite was still plain coffee. "Of course."

"And, uh…a London Fog latte, please."

For John, was left unspoken, but Chelsea's hand shook and she barely managed to keep from missing the cup and pouring the hot liquid over her other hand. "Sure."

After putting a lid on Callan's cup, she went through the process of making John's drink. Just the smell of it made her yearn for him, and she was glad she was able to keep her back to Callan for the most part. It wasn't easy to keep her emotions in check when she was this tired.

It had been almost two weeks since she told John they needed to break the habit of being in each other's company. The worst two weeks she'd had since losing her parents, actually. She'd deliberately put the distance between them in an effort to keep from getting hurt more than she already was—or to suffer through it lingering on and on—but it wasn't working.

When she put John's drink on the counter, Callan handed her a gift card. "I won this in a bet, so I may as well use it."

"Wait." Chelsea held up the card. "Was the bet with Chief Boudreaux? Margaret came in for the card and said he lost a bet, but that she wasn't at liberty to tell me what it was."

"Probably because, during a conversation about municipal services, I made a joke about the fact if I called 911, I bet the fire department would arrive before the police department and he took exception to it. So a bet was made, with coffee on the line."

"They're right next to each other," she pointed out, and he nodded. "Though, to be fair, the firefighters are generally at the station, while the police officers could be anywhere in town."

"It's not my fault he didn't define the parameters of the bet."

She laughed. "I'm afraid to ask how you settled the bet."

"It took weeks, actually. But remember that thankfully minor car accident in front of the library? I'm the one who called 911. And the fire truck arrived a solid four minutes before the police car."

"No wonder Margaret wasn't at liberty to share the details."

Callan chuckled. "He was pretty grumpy about it, for sure. I should get back next door. We're doing window displays with examples of some restored photographs and *somebody* is obsessed with everything being exactly level."

Somebody being John, of course, and she felt the familiar pang that tweaked her heart every time she thought about him. He was finally doing his window display, and even though she missed not being a part of it, she ached to see it. Maybe she could sneak past when she closed and see the photographs without spotting him through the glass. That was unlikely, but she already knew she was going to try.

"It'll look amazing when you're done, I'm sure," she said, knowing the smile she gave him was wooden, but it was the best she could do.

"I think so, too." He picked up the drinks and got halfway out the door, but then he paused and looked back at her. "I know lives and relationships are complicated, but Molly said something a few days ago that's been stuck in my head. You were both happy when you were together, and now neither of you are. Something to think about."

Once the door closed behind him, Chelsea let loose a howl of frustration and picked up her towel just so she could ball it up and throw it at the wall. It wasn't as satisfying as shattering a coffee mug, but it definitely caused less damage.

Something to think about?

It was *all* she thought about.

"How is she?" John took the London Fog latte from Callan, inhaling the aroma that would always make him think of Chelsea. "Also, thank you."

"Keeping in mind I'm neither psychic nor somebody who knows her well enough to know all her facial expressions and stuff, I'd say she's doing about the same as you. Miserable and trying to hide it. And failing."

John took a sip of the drink, not caring if he burned his mouth. It felt like the last connection he had with the woman who'd made it, and he was going to savor every drop of it.

"Are we almost done with this?" Callan asked, setting his coffee down on the edge of the desk.

John allowed the change in subject because he wasn't sure what he could say about Chelsea. He was going to need some time to wrap his mind around the fact she appeared miserable, as well. She was the one who'd cut off their relationship.

"We have four more pairs, I think."

They'd spent the morning slipping the before-and-after photos into the thin matted frames he'd bought, which then attached to the windows with a special adhesive. Time would tell how it stood up to radical temperature changes in the glass, but for now it looked amazing.

There were some personal photos—hung with permission of the clients, of course—that had been damaged by water or being folded. Some were quite old and were damaged by years of being carried in a wallet. There were a few landscape photos to highlight his ability to remove power lines and other scenery-ruining items. And he'd chosen a few of the historical photos he'd been working on for the library.

He was currently framing a sepia-toned photo of the gazebo in the town square, taken the day of its ribbon cutting. The original was the only known photograph left, and for whatever reason, it had been torn into four pieces and then taped back together. The tape was yellow, the corners were curling and it was a hot mess. It had been one of the most challenging of the town photos, but now Stonefield had a perfect copy celebrating one of their most beloved landmarks.

He ran his finger over the roofline of the gazebo. "This really is a beautiful town."

"Yeah, it is. It's a shame you're planning to leave it," Callan said. Before John could decide if he wanted to say the words out loud—*I don't think I want to leave anymore*—his friend continued. "It's kind of funny that I'm the flip side of that coin. I did a lot of research and chose this town deliberately. But you never really wanted to live here. You only came here to be close to your family, and you always planned to leave it. And us."

And Chelsea. But something in Callan's voice—like maybe his feelings were hurt—jerked his attention away from dwelling on her. "Callan, I—"

"No, I get it. I mean, you told me when we met you planned to be here for a year. But you were the first friend I made here *not* through Molly, and… well, I asked you to be my best man for a reason. But it's not like you're leaving the planet. We'll be in touch."

"I don't know what I'm doing."

Callan looked up from the photo he was trying to fit to the frame. "With regard to..."

John snorted. "My life? Lately, I've been trying to imagine leaving, and I can't see myself leaving Bruce, Ann-Marie and the girls, or you and Molly, or—of course—Chelsea."

His friend's face brightened. "So what's the problem?"

"I don't know if I can stay because... Chelsea."

"If you stay, doesn't that solve the problems between you two?"

John frowned. "I don't think so. I mean, she said it was no strings while I was staying with her, and then after we had dinner at the diner, she said we shouldn't be around each other anymore. She cut me loose."

Callan pressed his lips together and then, after a quick shake of his head, bent to the photograph again.

"What?" It occurred to John that Callan might have inside information on Chelsea's frame of mind due to being Molly's husband. If there way anybody in Stonefield Chelsea was going to confide in, it was Callan's wife. "Tell me."

A phone chimed, and Callan looked almost relieved when he picked his up off the desk and looked at the screen. "Oh, look at that. I have to go now. Sorry."

"Callan."

"I'm serious. The HVAC guy needs access to my office, which I keep locked."

"Afraid somebody's going to steal the overdue fine quarters?"

"Hey." Callan stood and slid his phone in his pocket. "It's a lot of quarters. The good people of Stonefield are not great at returning books."

Before Callan could reach the door, John stopped him. "Hey. Do you really think she's miserable?"

"I don't want to be in the middle of this, but I think you both need to stop navigating what you think the other person wants and be honest with yourselves and maybe with each other about what *you* want."

He was gone before John could make the decision to push harder—to find out what he knew that would make him say that. Had Chelsea told Molly something different than she'd told John?

An hour later the window was finished. His mind had spent the entire hour bouncing between going back to his home office to hide or going next door to talk to Chelsea. If she was as miserable as Callan thought, maybe she missed him as badly as he missed her. Maybe, despite what she said, there *were* strings attached. And she'd opened the door by sending the emoji last night. He could congratulate her on her favorite contestant winning Survivor.

But the ridiculousness of needing that flimsy excuse annoyed him. It shouldn't be this hard if they were on the same page, so clearly they weren't. And he had one job he wanted to finish before the end of the day.

A young man had brought in a family photo—

him, his mom and his former stepdad taken on the beach during a family vacation. It was his and his mother's favorite photo together, but the stepdad had turned out to be not very nice and though he was long gone, it had ruined the picture for them. Removing the stepdad from the picture wasn't hard, but it was fairly detailed work and the mother's birthday was in four days.

John lost track of time, as he often did when working pixel by pixel, and when he finally sent the file to his photo printer, his back was killing him. Groaning, he stretched and that was when he saw her.

Chelsea was standing outside, looking at the before-and-after photographs he'd displayed, just as she'd suggested. She leaned in to give one a closer look, her mouth curved into a smile.

John stood and took a few steps toward the door with no idea what he was going to do when he reached it. Maybe he'd just say hi. He could talk to her about the Survivor finale. Or he could pull her into his arms and kiss her until neither of them could breathe. He could tell her he loved her and that marrying her was not a mistake, but the best thing that had ever happened to him.

Then their eyes met through the window and for a few heartbeats, their gazes locked. It had been almost two weeks since he'd kissed her. He missed her face. Her smile. The sound of her voice. He'd just missed *her*, and she was right there on the other side of the glass.

Before he was halfway to her, though, she took a deep breath and broke the eye contact. Then she gave him a sad smile and walked away.

Chapter Twenty-Two

Sutton's Place Brewery & Tavern will be closed this Saturday for a private event, but if you stop in during their regular open hours and buy a $50 gift card, you'll get a $10 bonus gift card to keep or give away. Give your friends and family—and yourself—the gift of a night out this year!

—Stonefield Gazette *Facebook Page*

Just before Chelsea pulled the door to the Sutton's Place taproom open, Molly stopped her with a hand on her arm. "Hey. Try to embrace the jolly tonight, okay?"

"I'm here. I'm wearing my red dress. I'll smile and talk to people." But jolly? That was a promise she couldn't make.

It wasn't as if she hadn't been trying. The café was decorated. Customers were greeted with Christmas music, even though it was hard for her to listen to all day. She'd never realized how many pop Christmas songs were about holiday heartbreak until she'd had her own heart broken.

Being invited to the Sutton family's private Christmas party should have been a joyous occasion. She'd been waiting her entire life to be part of a community—to really belong—and she finally did. But now the only thing she felt was lonely. She missed John and she kept expecting—hoping—she would miss him less the next day. So far it wasn't happening.

"We're going to have fun," Callan said, snaking his arm past Chelsea to open the door for her. "And it's too cold for you two to stand around outside."

Chelsea stepped into the taproom and had to admit her spirits were instantly lifted as she was wrapped in warmth and laughter. Colored Christmas lights twinkled around the tops of the walls, and a massive tree stood in the back corner. The space was full of people she liked, and a night of festivity would do her good.

Ellen greeted them first. "I'm so glad to see you all! And you ladies look lovely, as always."

Chelsea slipped out of her coat, handing it to Callan to hang on the rack with Molly's. Then she ran her hand over the red dress, trying not to think about the last time she'd worn it. "Thank you for inviting me."

"Of course!" Ellen kissed her cheek and Chelsea had to rapidly blink back tears so she didn't embarrass herself. "Now, go enjoy yourself. It's an open bar tonight and there's food in the back."

Making her way through the taproom was like running a gauntlet of greetings. Laura and Riley. Gwen and Case. Evie and Mallory, whose husbands were behind the bar. Kids and babies. Molly's parents, Paul and Amanda. There were also people Chelsea only knew in passing or from their drink orders, but she smiled and said hello. The tree service employees were there, as well. Her heart pinched when she spotted Bruce and Ann-Marie across the room, and she turned, pretending she hadn't seen them.

Christmas music was playing, loud enough to be festive, but not so loud the guests had to yell to each other. Chelsea hummed along with a classic as she made her way toward the bar. Molly had told her Lane and Irish brewed up a special spiced ale for the holidays and she'd promised to try it.

Then she saw him.

John was leaning against the bar, glass in hand, watching people mingle. There was nowhere to hide as his head moved, and she knew he'd spot her any second.

When their eyes met, she saw his body stiffen. His jaw clenched, the muscles in his neck flexing. Just a hint of red colored the tops of his cheeks as his lips pressed together.

He didn't look happy to see her.

That was too bad. She wasn't just passing through, reconnecting with family before moving on to bigger pastures. Stonefield was her home and these people were the closest thing to family she'd had in a very long time. If one of them had to leave this party to avoid it being painfully awkward, it wasn't going to be her.

She also wasn't going to detour away from the bar just because he was standing there. After taking a shaky breath, she joined him. "Hi, John."

"Chelsea." He smiled. "Quite a party."

"The taproom's beautiful tonight."

Irish approached her, giving a rare—from him—smile. He set down a coaster with her name written on it in a sparkly, metallic paint. Evie's work, probably. "What can I get you, Chelsea?"

"I promised Molly I'd try the spiced ale."

"Good choice," he said, and a moment later he set a glass on the coaster in front of her before disappearing again.

She took a sip of the spiced ale and then smiled. "It's delicious, of course. I don't think it's possible for Lane and Irish to brew a bad beer."

John nodded and then turned his body toward hers, so close she could feel the warmth radiating from him. Then he bent so his mouth was close to her ear and she felt the heat of his breath on her neck. "You're wearing your wedding dress."

Chelsea shivered, barely resisting the urge to lean

into him. "It's a Christmas party and this is the only red dress I own."

"When you put it on, did you think about us?"

The words cut through her, making her gasp and leaving her unable to think fast enough to reply with anything but the truth. "I think about us all the time."

He was shifting closer and she felt the brush of his fingertips on her lower back, but she didn't have the strength to walk away from him. No matter how they'd started and no matter how they would inevitably end up, in this moment all she wanted to do was step into his arms and let him hold her.

"Dance with me," he said as the music changed, and then he held out his hand.

The seconds between reaching out his hand and Chelsea taking it were the longest of John's life. He felt every heartbeat—every shallow breath—until she nodded and their fingers touched.

As a sweet, acoustic version of "I'll Be Home For Christmas" filled the taproom, he led her into the area cleared for dancing. Several other couples were there, but he paid no attention to them.

Wrapping his arms around Chelsea felt like a holiday miracle, and he listened to the lyrics of the song as they began to sway to the music. All he wanted for Christmas was to go home again—home to Chelsea where he knew in his heart he belonged.

He buried his face in her hair, inhaling the scent

of her shampoo. Her fingertips pressed into his back and he wondered if she could feel him trembling.

"I miss you," he said, his lips close to her ear. "I miss your voice. Your laugh. Falling asleep with you in my arms. Watching movies and *Survivor* together. I miss everything about you, but mostly I just miss you sharing your life with me."

He shouldn't be doing this here, with everybody they knew around them, but he couldn't hold it in anymore because he knew when this night was over, they were each going to go home. Alone. And he needed her to know he didn't want that.

This time, he was going to tell her.

Chelsea didn't pull away. She turned her head slightly so he could hear her over the music. "I miss you, too. Every minute."

"We don't *have* to miss each other anymore."

She did lift her head then, and their eyes met. "What are you saying? What about moving to the city—Concord or Portsmouth? You know I don't want to leave here."

John gave up all pretense of dancing. He took her face in his hands, looking into her eyes. "I'm not going anywhere. Everything I want is here. You. *Us*. I love you, Chelsea."

Her lips parted as her breath caught. "You do?"

"I do." He brushed a strand of hair from her cheek, his stomach in knots as he waited for her reaction.

"That's not the first time you've said *I do* to me," she said, her eyes sparkling. "But you better mean it this time, because I love you, too, John Fletcher. And I never dreamed it was possible those words would ever come out of my mouth, but they're the truest thing I've ever said."

His heart was going to burst. There was no way it could pound this hard and not explode. "Do you want to stay married to me?"

"I do."

He had to let her go in order to reach into his pocket and pull out the rings he always had with him now. She smiled, tears running down her cheeks, and reached out her hand. Their hands shook together as he slid the gold band onto her finger.

"For better or worse," he said, and he had to pause to clear the lump from his throat. "I promise to be there for you, no matter what. I'll be your rock—your *home*—and I'll love you for the rest of my life."

He could hear the sighs and sniffles around them, but he didn't take his eyes off Chelsea as she took the other band and worked it over his knuckle.

"John, I—" Her voice broke and she paused, taking a deep breath. "I love you. You already *are* my home. I promise to be your ride-or-die alliance and I'll *never* vote you off my island."

John lifted her off her feet as she wrapped her arms around his neck and kissed him. He could feel her smiling against his mouth, and it took a while for him to register the whistles and applause around them.

When he set her down, she kept hold of his neck. "Merry Christmas, husband."

"Merry Christmas, wife." It felt so damn good to say that. "And just think, forty years from now somebody in this town is going to say 'Remember when John and Chelsea made a spectacle of themselves kissing in the middle of the Suttons' Christmas party?' and we'll all laugh."

Her eyes softened. "I can't wait."

Somebody was touching his arm, probably wanting to congratulate them, but he leaned in and put his mouth close to Chelsea's ear so nobody else could hear the question he asked her.

"Do you think it's too late to ask for that toaster oven back?"

Epilogue

One year later...

The taproom of Sutton's Place Brewery & Tavern was full, which was quite a feat considering they were closed.

Chelsea let the warmth of the twinkling lights and the soft Christmas music mingling with voices and laughter wash over her. John's arm was around her shoulders and he squeezed lightly.

"You're sure you're up to this?" he asked, his mouth close to her ear.

She ran her hand over the swell of her stomach. "She's not due for another month. I'll be fine."

Molly spotted them first and wrapped her in a fierce hug. "Merry Christmas!"

"Are there even more people here than there were last year?" she asked. "Ellen's collecting people, isn't she?"

"Always."

"I'm so glad we're two of them." She laughed and reached for John's hand. "Or two and a half of them, I should say."

Callan walked over and shook John's hand before hugging Chelsea. "Merry Christmas. And I should thank you for being so very pregnant because I drank your share of the spiced ale."

"Hey," John said. "I thought what's my wife's is also *mine*. You drank *my* share of the spiced ale."

Callan shrugged. "Lane said they brewed twice as much this year, so they shouldn't run out. Maybe. I also drank everybody else's share, too."

"Our librarian is enjoying himself," Gwen said, shifting her son to her other arm so she could give Chelsea a one-armed hug. "We should pick the next Books & Brews book before he sobers up."

Case put his arm around Gwen's shoulders and kissed the top of his son's head. "I'm almost afraid of him picking a book drunk. We've seen how boring they are when he's sober enough to at least try to make them interesting."

"My friend Roman suggested a fascinating history of the financial district that—"

"Nope." Molly took her husband's arm and started leading him away. "Time to get some water into this guy."

Chelsea managed to bend enough to give Boomer's head a good scratching. The dog wasn't really supposed to be in the taproom, but it was a private function and Case and Gwen's dog was one of the most beloved members of the community. They couldn't leave him off the guest list.

"You should check out the food table. Laura finally perfected the most amazing snickerdoodle recipe ever," Molly said. "I need to go refill the punch bowl because Jack and Eli hit it pretty hard when they got here. They're banned from it now because two teens on a sugar high is a lot for one party."

They didn't go in a straight line to the food table, though. There were too many people to say hello to. John kept his hand at the small of her back as they greeted friends and family. Bruce and Ann-Marie had left Jenny and Carrie with a sitter even though they'd been invited, choosing instead to make the Christmas party their annual dress-up date night.

An hour into the event, John got into a conversation with Bruce and Riley, and Chelsea wandered away. Looking for a quiet corner, she found Ellen sitting alone, watching the party.

When Ellen noticed her and patted the empty chair next to her, Chelsea sat with a sigh of relief. "Thank you. I'm so used to being on my feet that sometimes I don't realize how tired I am until I sit down."

"You have help now, though. You need to take care of yourself."

"I've cut back now that Carla's confident she can handle everything. It still feels strange to sleep in, though."

Ellen laughed. "Honey, sleep all you can right now."

"I'm trying, believe me."

"I heard John's giving up the office space to be at home with the baby?"

"He is. I'll get up at four and open the café and work until ten Monday through Friday. When Carla comes in, I'll go home and John will go to his home office until dinner. We're going to try that for a while. And Carla's daughter wants to work, too, so they'll figure out afternoons and weekends themselves."

"And you know if you need a little time to yourselves, you can always drop the little one off with me for a while. To be honest, we probably wouldn't even notice one more."

"Thank you. We're grateful to have so many wonderful people in our lives." She leaned back and rested a hand on her stomach. "And most of them are here right now. It's a beautiful party."

Ellen nodded. "David would have loved this so much."

Chelsea hadn't known David Sutton, but she knew the story of how he and Lane Thompson had decided to turn their shared passion for brewing into a business. They'd been in too deep to back out when David passed away, though. "I'm sorry he passed away before he got to see it."

"Thank you. Me, too." Ellen sighed, and then she

looked around the room with a warm smile. "But you know if he'd lived, I don't think Gwen and Evie would have come home. It's not the taps and tables he would have loved, but the gathering of our friends and family. And seeing our daughters together, and our grandchildren… When I get sad missing him, I feel this warm glow of joy like a hug, and I know my David's watching over us."

"He would be so happy to see you all together. And there's so much love in this room."

"Speaking of love, here comes yours."

Chelsea turned and saw John coming toward them. He leaned down and kissed Ellen's cheek before turning to his wife. "I was going to ask for a dance, but I'm happy to see you off your feet."

"Oh, I want to dance with you." There was nothing she wanted more. She hoped dancing with her husband at the Suttons' Christmas party would be their holiday tradition for many years to come.

"Go and dance," Ellen said, pushing herself to her feet. "I'm going to see if any of my grandbabies need cuddling."

As John led her to the area for dancing, she saw him nod at Molly, who was standing near the sound system. As the song that had been playing came to an end, she hit a button and the soft opening notes of "I'll Be Home For Christmas" filled the taproom.

John pulled her into his arms and they began to sway in time to the music. Then they laughed when the baby kicked hard, clearly not liking him being against Chelsea's stomach.

"She wants to dance, too," he said.

"Trust me, she dances *plenty*." Chelsea rested her head against John's chest, even though her stomach made it slightly awkward, and smiled when he kissed her hair. "I love you."

"I love you, too." His hand rubbed her back. "And there's nothing I want for Christmas but to keep loving you. And in the New Year, bringing our daughter home."

Home. Chelsea's eyes welled up with happy tears, and she blinked them away. "I think we should leave the tree up until she gets here."

"Then we will. Anything you want."

She tilted her head back so she could see her husband's face. "I have everything I want."

We'll be taking time off as we enjoy Christmas with our loved ones, so there will be fewer posts from us. During the week between Christmas Day and New Year's Day, we'll be making plans for the New Year and enjoying the bright, snow-filled days—we hope—before we turn the corner into the bitterly cold months of January and February. Chief Bordeaux and Chief Nelson would like to remind us all to be safe and only drive sober. This holiday season, designated drivers get free coffee or soda at

Sutton's Place Brewery & Tavern, as well as an order of nachos.

Be kind to each other. Take care of your neighbors. Hold your loved ones close and laugh more than you cry. Have that second slice of pie. Happy holidays and best wishes!

—Stonefield Gazette *Facebook Page*

* * * * *

COMING NEXT MONTH FROM

◈ HARLEQUIN
SPECIAL EDITION

#3025 A TEMPORARY TEXAS ARRANGEMENT
Lockharts Lost & Found • by Cathy Gillen Thacker

Noah Lockhart, a widowed father of three girls, has vowed never to be reckless in love again...until he meets Tess Gardner, the veterinarian caring for his pregnant miniature donkey. But will love still be a possibility when one of his daughters objects to the romance?

#3026 THE AIRMAN'S HOMECOMING
The Tuttle Sisters of Coho Cove • by Sabrina York

As a former ParaJumper for the elite air force paramedic rescue wing, loner Noah Crocker has overcome enormous odds in his life. But convincing no-nonsense bakery owner Amy Tuttle Tolliver that he's ready to settle down with her and her sons may be his toughest challenge yet!

#3027 WRANGLING A FAMILY
Aspen Creek Bachelors • by Kathy Douglass

Before meeting Alexandra Jamison, rancher Nathan Montgomery never had time for romance. Now he needs a girlfriend in order to keep his matchmaking mother off his back, and single mom Alexandra fits the bill. If only their romance ruse didn't lead to knee-weakening kisses...

#3028 SAY IT LIKE YOU MEAN IT
by Rochelle Alers

When former actress Shannon Younger comes face-to-face with handsome celebrity landscape architect Joaquin Williamson, she vows not to come under his spell. She starts to trust Joaquin, but she knows that falling for another high-profile man could cost her her career—and her heart.

#3029 THEIR ACCIDENTAL HONEYMOON
Once Upon a Wedding • by Mona Shroff

Rani Mistry and Param Sheth have been besties since elementary school. When Param's wedding plans come to a crashing halt, they both go on his honeymoon—as friends. But when friendship takes a sharp turn into a marriage of convenience, will they fake it till they make it?

#3030 AN UPTOWN GIRL'S COWBOY
by Sasha Summers

Savannah Barrett is practically Texas royalty—a good girl with a guarded heart. But one wild night with rebel cowboy Angus McCarrick has her wondering if the boy her daddy always warned her about might be the Prince Charming she's always yearned for.

YOU CAN FIND MORE INFORMATION ON UPCOMING HARLEQUIN TITLES, FREE EXCERPTS AND MORE AT HARLEQUIN.COM.

HSECNM1123

Get 3 FREE REWARDS!

We'll send you 2 FREE Books <u>plus</u> a FREE Mystery Gift.

FREE Value Over **$20**

Both the **Harlequin® Special Edition** and **Harlequin® Heartwarming™** series feature compelling novels filled with stories of love and strength where the bonds of friendship, family and community unite.

YES! Please send me 2 FREE novels from the Harlequin Special Edition or Harlequin Heartwarming series and my FREE Gift (gift is worth about $10 retail). After receiving them, if I don't wish to receive any more books, I can return the shipping statement marked "cancel." If I don't cancel, I will receive 6 brand-new Harlequin Special Edition books every month and be billed just $5.49 each in the U.S. or $6.24 each in Canada, a savings of at least 12% off the cover price, or 4 brand-new Harlequin Heartwarming Larger-Print books every month and be billed just $6.24 each in the U.S. or $6.74 each in Canada, a savings of at least 19% off the cover price. It's quite a bargain! Shipping and handling is just 50¢ per book in the U.S. and $1.25 per book in Canada.* I understand that accepting the 2 free books and gift places me under no obligation to buy anything. I can always return a shipment and cancel at any time by calling the number below. The free books and gift are mine to keep no matter what I decide.

Choose one: ☐ **Harlequin Special Edition** (235/335 BPA GRMK)   ☐ **Harlequin Heartwarming Larger-Print** (161/361 BPA GRMK)   ☐ **Or Try Both!** (235/335 & 161/361 BPA GRPZ)

Name (please print)

Address   Apt. #

City   State/Province   Zip/Postal Code

Email: Please check this box ☐ if you would like to receive newsletters and promotional emails from Harlequin Enterprises ULC and its affiliates. You can unsubscribe anytime.

Mail to the Harlequin Reader Service:
IN U.S.A.: P.O. Box 1341, Buffalo, NY 14240-8531
IN CANADA: P.O. Box 603, Fort Erie, Ontario L2A 5X3

Want to try 2 free books from another series? Call 1-800-873-8635 or visit www.ReaderService.com.

*Terms and prices subject to change without notice. Prices do not include sales taxes, which will be charged (if applicable) based on your state or country of residence. Canadian residents will be charged applicable taxes. Offer not valid in Quebec. This offer is limited to one order per household. Books received may not be as shown. Not valid for current subscribers to the Harlequin Special Edition or Harlequin Heartwarming series. All orders subject to approval. Credit or debit balances in a customer's account(s) may be offset by any other outstanding balance owed by or to the customer. Please allow 4 to 6 weeks for delivery. Offer available while quantities last.

Your Privacy—Your information is being collected by Harlequin Enterprises ULC, operating as Harlequin Reader Service. For a complete summary of the information we collect, how we use this information and to whom it is disclosed, please visit our privacy notice located at corporate.harlequin.com/privacy-notice. From time to time we may also exchange your personal information with reputable third parties. If you wish to opt out of this sharing of your personal information, please visit readerservice.com/consumerschoice or call 1-800-873-8635. **Notice to California Residents**—Under California law, you have specific rights to control and access your data. For more information on these rights and how to exercise them, visit corporate.harlequin.com/california-privacy.

HSEHW23